*Remembering You*

Sandi Lynn

*Sandi Lynn*

Remembering You

Copyright © 2014 Sandi Lynn Romance, L.L.C.

Cover Design by Cassy Roop @ Pink Ink Designs

Stock Photo: 84114878

Photographer: kiuikson

www.dollarphotoclub.com

Editing by B.Z. Hercules

I believe in the immeasurable power of love, that true love can endure any circumstance and reach across any distance.

~Dr. Steven Maraboli

When it's time for souls to meet, there's nothing on Earth that can prevent them from meeting, no matter where each may be located.

~Kushandwi Zoom

## *Table of Contents*

## *Prologue*

They say young love isn't real. It's only our bodies, full of raging hormones, and our minds filled with lust that make us think we are in love. I can tell them they're wrong. Young love is real; it can, and it does exist, at least in my seventeen-year-old life.

"You are not to see that boy anymore!" Corrine yelled as she followed me up the stairs.

"Mom, stop! You don't even know him."

"I know enough not to like him." She chased after me.

I stepped into my bedroom and turned towards the door. "You don't like him because he's not rich, and he doesn't live in a big, fancy house," I snapped.

Corrine followed me into my room. "He's not good enough for you, and I don't want you seeing him."

"Really, Mother? Are you worried that I'll tarnish your reputation, give your friends something to talk about, or, better yet, that I'll disgrace the Montgomery name?"

"Claire, that's not fair!" she snapped.

"Not fair?" I yelled. "What's not fair is you judging Sam for where he comes from instead of getting to know him as a person."

"This discussion is over and so is your relationship," she yelled as she turned on her heels and stomped out of my room.

Tears started to sting my eyes as I lay on my bed, looking at the picture of us on my phone. Sam was perfect to me and I loved him. I just wished I could make my mother and father see that.

# *Chapter 1*

Harry and Corinne Montgomery. What can I say? Harry was a doctor, a plastic surgeon, to be exact, and he was the best in Orange County. Corinne, my mother, spent her time, when not trying to run my life, doing charity work for different charities. Sometimes, people mistook us for sisters. She didn't look like she was forty-five, but more like thirty. I guess it helped when your husband was a plastic surgeon. Her best feature was her long, dark auburn hair, which complemented her emerald eyes. Harry and I had the same eyes: icy blue like the sea. Both of my parents were snobs in every sense of the word. They judged people based on what they didn't have instead of seeing them for who they were. I kept asking them if I was adopted because I was so different. I was not materialistic, and big expensive things didn't matter to me as much as they did to my parents and Zoey.

My sister, Zoey, was a Mini-Me of Corinne; they shared the same color hair and emerald eyes and, at the age of twenty-one, she was engaged to a senator's son. She'd had her eyes set on him since she was sixteen years old. The Desmonds were one of the most influential families in California, and Zoey was making sure she became a part of that. What Zoey didn't know was how Dylan Desmond, her beloved fiancé, tried to have sex with me last year. I told him, for his sake, I wouldn't tell my sister, but he'd better never come within six feet of me again or I would start a scandal, not only for what he tried with me, but with all the other women he had on the side. I had pictures of him that he didn't even know about. Half the time, he wouldn't even look at me anymore, which was the way I liked it.

Zoey spent a lot of her time criticizing me for the way I dressed; apparently, jeans and a t-shirt weren't her thing. She didn't like to tell people we were sisters because she was embarrassed of me. Corinne didn't stick up for me either; she would just tell Zoey to be nice and then the two of them would start to discuss the wedding. I didn't really care, though; my family was from a different world and it was a world I didn't belong in.

I was the quiet type. I had two best friends, Ally and Rachel, whom I'd known since kindergarten. My passion was reading and I liked to get lost in a good book. It was my escape from my family. Another one of my passions was Sam Snow.

Sam and I met when my car broke down and I was standing on the side of the road trying to call Corinne or Harry, but neither one answered. Sam was driving a tow truck when he saw me and he pulled over to ask if I needed help. The moment he opened the door and got out of his truck, I knew my life would never be the same. He was the hottest guy I'd ever seen. He stood about six-foot-two with a muscular build. He wore his sandy brown hair short and spikey in a messy kind of way, but very sexy, and his eyes were a blue-gray that were mesmerizing to look at.

"Hey, do you need some help?" the handsome stranger asked me as he walked towards me.

"Um, my car broke down, and I've been trying to call my parents with no luck."

He smiled at me and my knees started shaking. No one should ever be this beautiful.

"Looks like it's your lucky day. I can give you and your car a lift to my garage. It's over in Irvine."

I really had no choice but to go with him. Should I have been scared? Maybe I should have been, but I wasn't. There was something about him that made me feel safe. I felt things in my body that I'd never felt before when he looked at me.

"Thank you. I really appreciate it." I smiled.

He looked down as if he were embarrassed, as the smile never left his face. "Okay, let's get your car hooked up. You can wait in the truck."

I nodded my head and got in. Once he had my car hooked up, he climbed in and sat beside me. He turned and looked at me with those amazing eyes and held out his hand, "Hi, I'm Sam Snow."

I bit my bottom lip as I smiled back. "I'm Claire Montgomery."

The charge that went through my body when we touched was amazing; it was like I came alive. He started the truck and headed towards Irvine. The radio was on and the song "Yellow" by Coldplay played through the speakers. "I love this song," I said.

Sam looked at me as he turned it up. "I do too. Coldplay is my favorite band of all time."

"Shut up!" I exclaimed as I looked at him. "They're my favorite band too."

He laughed softly and the rest of the ride to Irvine was made up of us talking about all the other music we had in common.

When we reached Cal's Towing and Fixit Place, I got out of the truck as Sam backed up the car into an empty stall and unhooked it. I walked around, trying to call Corrine and Harry again, but still no answer. So I tried, against my better judgment, Zoey.

"Hello, Claire. What do you want?" she asked in an irritated manner.

"Can you come get me? My car broke down. I had to have it towed and now I need a ride home." I heard a sigh.

"Where are you?" she asked.

"I'm at a place called Cal's Towing in Irvine."

"Irvine!" she yelled. "Listen, I'm with Dylan right now and we are looking at invitations for the engagement party. You'll have to wait a couple of hours or call a cab."

"A cab? I'm not calling a cab. You're my sister, and I can't get a hold of Mom or Dad."

Sam was standing in front of me, listening to my conversation with my stuck up, self-absorbed sister. He motioned to me that he would give me a ride home.

"Claire, stop being a baby," she proceeded to say as I hung up and sighed.

"You don't have to worry. I can give you a ride home." He smiled as he looked down and lightly kicked the dirt with the toe of his boot.

Every time he smiled, I felt weak in the knees. "I don't want you to go out of your way; you've done so much for me already and I don't want to be a burden."

"It's not a problem at all, and you're no burden. Please don't think like that."

I looked down in embarrassment. "It's just that my family is really busy with their lives and, well—"

Sam bent over so his face was looking at mine. "I want to drive you home, Claire."

I gave him a small smile. He wasn't the only shy one here. "Okay, then I accept."

I filled out some paperwork for the repairs on my car as Sam grabbed his keys.

"Hey, Cal, Claire doesn't have a ride, so I'm going to give her a lift home. I'll be back soon."

"Okay, Sam. It was nice to meet you, Claire." Cal waved.

"Nice to meet you too." I waved with a smile.

\*\*\*\*

Sam's car was a black 1967 Chevy Impala. He walked over to the passenger's door and opened it for me. So far, he seemed to be a perfect gentleman.

"Nice wheels you have here."

"Thanks. This baby is my pride and joy." He smiled.

"Is there a story behind it?"

"I'll tell you on the way home, but first, you need to tell me where you live."

A sick feeling settled into my stomach. I didn't want to tell him I lived in Newport Beach for fear he would think I was one of those stuck-up rich girls. I started sliding my teeth along my bottom lip as I whispered, "Newport Beach."

He leaned a little closer to me and whispered, "What did you say?"

I let out a little laugh. "Newport Beach; please don't judge me." The words fell out of my mouth.

Sam cocked his head to the side. "Why would I judge you?"

I let out a sigh. "Because people normally judge people from Newport Beach."

The corners of his mouth turned up slightly. "Sounds like you're ashamed of living there."

I shrugged my shoulders. "Let's just say I'd rather live somewhere else. Now tell me about this baby of yours."

I needed to change the subject. It was bad enough he was going to see my mansion of a house and how I lived. I could see his blue-gray eyes light up as he was about to tell me.

"Someone had it towed to the garage. It hadn't run in years and it was rusting out. Cal told me if I could fix and restore it, the car was mine."

"Wow, that was very generous of him," I said.

He showed a small smile. "Yeah, he's kind of been like a father figure to me for a few years."

I could see a hurt in his face when he said that, but I didn't ask any more questions because it wasn't my business.

"Open the glove box," he said.

I pushed the button and opened it. Inside, there was a CD in a case that was labeled "Coldplay." I looked over at him, and we both smiled at each other.

"You can put it in," he said.

I took the CD out of the case and popped it in the CD player. "Fix You" was the first song to grace the speakers of the 1967 Chevy Impala. We drove, listened, and sang all the way to my house.

When Sam turned into the long, winding driveway of the house, I could see the look on his face as he pulled up to the mansion.

"Wow, this is really nice, Claire," he said as he hunched over the steering wheel to get a better look.

I shrugged. "It's okay."

He got out, walked around, and opened the door for me. That was the one thing that amazed me most about Sam.

"Thank you, Sam, for helping me today. I want to repay you somehow."

He put his hands in his pockets and looked down at the ground. He did that quite a bit.

"You could have dinner with me sometime," he whispered.

I leaned into him and whispered, "What did you say?"

He looked up at me and chuckled. "I said you can have dinner with me sometime."

A huge smile beamed across my face. "I would love to have dinner with you."

He smiled back as he fidgeted. "How about tomorrow night? I can pick you up at seven o'clock."

"Sounds great. I'll be ready."

The smile never left his face as he walked over to his car, gave me a wave, and drove away.

As I watched him pull away, my phone rang and Zoey's name appeared. "Hello," I snapped as I walked up the walkway.

"Do you still need us to pick you up?"

"No, I'm home now. Sorry to have inconvenienced you," I said as I hit the end button.

I walked into the mansion and started walking up to my room when I heard Corrine call my name.

"I saw you tried to call me a billion times, Claire. What was so important?"

I abruptly stopped in place and turned around to face her. "Why didn't you answer, Mother?"

"I was in a charity meeting, and I couldn't talk."

"Well, my car broke down, and I was stranded on the side of the road. But don't worry. A nice man stopped, offered me some candy, and when I accepted, he gave me a lift to a garage."

Her eyes widened. "Claire, you could have been raped or kidnapped. What have I told you about strangers? Why didn't you call your sister?"

"I did call Zoey, but she was too busy with her dog of a fiancé to pick me up."

"Claire, that isn't nice to say about Dylan."

I stomped up the stairs because this conversation was over as far as I was concerned.

"Where's your car?" she yelled.

"Don't worry about it. It's being repaired, and I can pick it up tomorrow." I went to my room and slammed my door, then fell across my bed and fell asleep.

# *Chapter 2*

I awoke a couple of hours later to someone banging on my door.

"Claire, it's dinner time," Zoey yelled.

Another wonderful family dinner; the four of us sitting around the table talking about our day. Oh wait, the conversation would be between Corinne and Zoey and about the engagement party, wedding, or a new clothing designer they just discovered. I rolled my eyes and headed down the stairs. I walked over to Harry, who was already seated in the dining room and kissed him on the cheek.

"Hi, Dad." I smiled.

"Hi, Claire. How was your day? Sorry I couldn't answer your call, but I was in surgery all day."

"It's fine, Dad. No worries."

"I didn't think you were home. I didn't see your car in the driveway," he said.

"It broke down today. I had it towed and it's being fixed."

"Broke down? See, Claire, that's why I wanted to buy you a new car and not have you drive that old one."

"Dad, the car is only six years old, and I like my Volkswagen Bug."

Harry rolled his eyes as Corinne and Zoey walked in and set dinner on the table. I glanced at Zoey and turned away. I had nothing to say to her ever again for leaving me stranded, not that I minded, because Sam wouldn't have driven me home and we probably wouldn't be going on a date tomorrow night, but it was an excuse for me to be mad at her.

"Oh, don't look at me like that, Claire. If you would have let Daddy buy you a *new* car, you wouldn't have been in that predicament."

"Shut up, Zoey. You sound stupid," I snapped.

"Mom, are you going to let her call me that?" she whined.

Corinne sighed. "Claire, what is the matter with you? Why can't you get along with your sister? I'm sorry your car broke down, but she has a point. If you had a new car that wouldn't have happened."

I looked down and didn't say another word. I learned that it wasn't worth it when it came to Zoey. Harry spoke up. "The point is, Claire made it home all right and she's safe." He winked at me.

"How did you get home?" Corinne asked.

"The man from the garage overheard my bitchy sister refusing to come get me and offered me a ride home." I smiled because I knew that would get under Corinne's and Zoey's skin.

"Well," she mumbled. "I'll have to thank that man for seeing you got home safely but he could have been a murderer, Claire."

Okay, ready? Here's where Corinne's going to flip.

"You can thank him tomorrow. He asked me to go out to dinner with him." I smiled.

Corinne put down her fork and glared at me across the table.

"Did you put a spell on him or something?" Zoey laughed.

"Zoey, shut up!" I yelled.

"Claire, I don't think it's a good idea. How old is this man?"

"He's nineteen, Mom, and before you ask, he did graduate high school."

"Does he work at that garage for a living?"

I could see the disgust in her face as she asked me.

"Yes. He's a mechanic, and he's going to fix my car."

Zoey rolled her eyes. "Ew, a grease monkey."

I balled my left fist because I was going to jump across the table and deck her right in her pretty little face. Harry looked at me and saw what was going on. He yelled at her to be quiet. Corinne looked down and didn't say another word. I quietly got up, grabbed my plate, and put it in the kitchen sink.

"Look what the two of you have done; you both should be ashamed of yourselves," Harry said.

I quietly took the back stairs to my room. I picked up my phone from the bed and saw that I had a text message from a number I didn't recognize.

*"Hi, Claire, it's Sam. I hope you don't mind, but I took your number from the repair slip at the shop. I just wanted to tell you that I'm looking forward to dinner tomorrow night."*

I smiled like a kid on Christmas morning as I replied back.

*"Hi, Sam. I don't mind at all. In fact, I'm glad you did. I look forward to having dinner with you tomorrow too."*

A few seconds later, another text from Sam came through.

*"Great. I'll see you tomorrow. Bye, Claire."*

My heart fluttered and excitement settled through my body. I took a shower and climbed into bed, looking out the window at the sky that was lit up from the stars and thinking about Sam.

****

The next morning, my alarm went off at six for school. My best friends, Rachel and Ally, were picking me up, since my car was being repaired. I put on a pair of skinny jeans, my Coldplay t-shirt, and threw my long, light brown hair in a ponytail. This was usually my everyday school look. It smelled like pancakes throughout the house, and since I didn't eat dinner last night, I was starving. I walked down the back stairs into the kitchen to find Harry flipping pancakes.

"Good morning, sweetheart." He smiled.

"Morning, Dad," I said as I gently placed my hand on his shoulder. "Smells good in here. Are those your famous apple cinnamon pancakes?"

"Yep, and I made them just for you." He winked.

I poured a cup of coffee and perched myself on a stool at the island. Harry put two large pancakes on my plate and set the bottle of syrup on the counter. Corinne and Zoey walked in.

"Oh, Harry, these smell wonderful." She smiled as she kissed him on the cheek.

Zoey looked at me and snarled, "You're going to get fat."

I cut a large piece of my pancake, picked it up with my hand, shoved it in my mouth, and looked at her while chewing slowly.

"Claire, that's enough!" Corinne snapped.

"Good morning to you too, Mom," I said with a mouthful.

Harry looked at Zoey. "Claire weighs about ninety pounds. She could stand to put on a little weight. Leave her alone."

There was one thing I could always count on and that was Harry to be on my side. He sat down next to me at the island.

"I was thinking, why don't you ask this new friend of yours to come to the house for dinner tonight?"

I started choking on my pancakes. "Dad, no offense, but I just met him. I'm not ready to have him dragged through the mud from the likes of this family."

"Claire, we wouldn't do that," he said.

"Oh, the hell you wouldn't. I have to go to school. I'll see you later, Dad." I got up, kissed him on the cheek, glared at Zoey, and said goodbye to Corinne.

Rachel and Ally were waiting for me outside. I hopped into the back seat and sighed. Ally turned around and looked at me.

"Another Montgomery family breakfast?"

I rolled my eyes. "Yes, the usual bullshit."

"So what happened to the Bug?" Rachel asked.

"It just broke down, and I'm going on a date tonight." I smiled.

Ally whipped her head around to face me. "What? Claire Montgomery doesn't date."

"I know, I know, keep your panties on," I said as I bit down on my lip.

"Come on, Claire, we haven't got all day. Spill," Rachel snapped.

"His name is Sam, and he was driving his tow truck yesterday and saw me standing on the side of the road next to my car. He pulled over and offered to help me. He took my car to his garage, drove me home, and asked me to go to dinner with him."

Ally pounded her fists on her knees. "OMG, OMG, I can't believe it. He's like Prince Charming coming to your rescue."

I smiled. "He's really nice. He's such a gentleman, and we both love Coldplay."

"Well, there's a match made in Heaven." Rachel laughed.

We pulled into the parking lot at school and Ally grabbed my arm. "What's Corinne going to say, Claire? He works in a garage; he's not a millionaire."

"She already knows and is pissed. But I don't care, because when I was with him, I felt alive for the first time in my life."

Rachel stopped and looked at me. "What do you mean?"

"All I know is when I was with him, I felt something I never felt before. I was so happy and I felt safe. I felt like I could conquer the world."

Ally rolled her eyes. "Stop being dramatic and let's get to class."

It was the truth, and I knew nobody could relate to what I was feeling. I just hoped I wasn't headed for heartbreak.

# *Chapter 3*

The day seemed to last forever, and I couldn't wait to get out of school. I didn't have much time left. I was graduating in a month and then I was heading off to the University of Washington to study Journalism and Literature. As soon as I got home, I ran upstairs and got in the shower. I liked my showers scolding hot and had a habit of staying in too long. I stood under the hot water and washed my hair, thinking about Sam and how I couldn't wait to see him. I was confused because I'd never felt this way about a person before. Guys had always been interested in me, but I'd never found any of them interesting enough to date. They were all spoiled rich boys that were used to getting everything they wanted. I stepped out of the shower, pruned skin and all, wrapped a towel around me, and heard my phone chime. I grabbed my phone from my purse and saw there was a text from Sam.

*"Hi, Claire, your car will be ready sometime tomorrow. I had to order a part and it won't be in until tomorrow morning. I wanted to keep you updated. See you tonight."*

*"Thank you, Sam. I'm looking forward to our date,"* I replied back.

*"Me too, Claire,"* he replied with a smiley face.

My heart started to flutter when I saw his text. I wondered if he had been thinking about me all day like I was thinking about him. I put on a pair of skinny black jeans and a pale pink lace tank top with a matching cami underneath. As I was getting dressed, there was a knock at my door.

"Claire, it's us. Can we come in?" Ally said.

"Yeah, it's open. Come in."

The door flew open and Ally and Rachel strolled in with a duffel bag. "We're here to help you get ready for your date." Rachel smiled.

"I can get ready on my own, thank you." I smiled.

Ally walked over and grabbed my hands. "Claire, this is your first date ever, and we, as your best friends, are going to make sure you look hot!"

Rachel threw the duffel bag on my bed and started unloading the massive amounts of hair products, curling irons, and makeup. Ally walked me over to my vanity and pointed to the chair, ordering me to sit down. She did my makeup while Rachel curled my hair. Once I was finished, I looked in the mirror, and even I couldn't believe what I saw. Rachel curled my hair so the curls flowed softly around my shoulders and Ally did my eyes in a smoky color with a bit of blush and a light pink lipstick. I must admit, I looked good and, for the first time, I felt sexy.

I glanced at my phone and it was 6:45 p.m. when we walked downstairs. Ally and Rachel said they weren't leaving until they met Sam. I could tell they were dying to see what he looked like. I walked into the kitchen to grab a bottle of water and Corinne and Zoey were sitting at the table, looking through wedding magazines. Both of them looked up. The expression on Zoey's face was priceless.

"Claire, you look absolutely beautiful." Corinne smiled. "Zoey, doesn't your sister look amazing?"

"Yeah, she's okay," she said.

The doorbell rang and, instantly, the butterflies awoke from their dormant sleep and started fluttering around. I tried to run to the door before anyone else could, but it was too late; Rachel had already let Sam in and both her and Ally were already drooling over him.

"Sam, hi." I smiled.

"Hi, Claire. Wow, you look amazing."

I bit my bottom lip and looked down. "Thank you. I see you have met my two best friends."

"Yes, I have." Sam laughed.

The dreaded moment came when I saw Zoey and Corinne standing in the doorway between the hall and the kitchen.

"Sam, this is my mother, Corinne, and my sister, Zoey," I introduced.

Sam walked over to them and held out his hand. "Nice to meet you both."

Zoey looked him up and down, and Corinne lightly shook his hand. I needed to get him out of there as fast I could.

"Come on, Sam. Let's go. I'm starving."

He looked at me and smiled. "I'm ready when you are."

We walked outside, and I turned back to look at Ally and Rachel, who were both standing there with their jaws dropped open. "OMG, he's a dream God," Ally mouthed as Rachel gave a thumbs up.

He opened the car door for me and I slid in. "What's your favorite type of food?" Sam asked.

"Hmm, I like all kinds of food, but if you must know, my absolute favorite is Mexican."

His eyes lit up like lightning in the sky. "Mine too. I'd like to take you to my favorite Mexican restaurant, if that's okay."

"I'd like that very much." I smiled.

We pulled up to Diablo's, a Mexican restaurant that was also my favorite.

"I love this place; they have the best Mexican food."

"You know Diablos?" he asked.

"Yep, I first came here with Rachel and her family. I've been addicted to it ever since."

We walked in the restaurant and were seated at a table near the fireplace. The décor was amazing. The walls were painted with murals of cities in Mexico while the ceiling was covered in clouds. The waiter came by with chips and salsa and asked us for our drink order. I opened the menu, but already knew what I was getting. Diablos had the best Mexican pizza.

"What do you usually get?" I asked Sam.

He glanced up from his menu. "Either the Mexican pizza or the chicken enchiladas."

I smiled as my heart started to beat a little faster. "The Mexican pizza is my favorite."

"Looks like we have a lot in common, Claire," he said as he gently put his hand on mine and then looked down.

I didn't pull away; I loved the way his skin felt on mine. During dinner, we held deep discussions about our families. Sam's dad had passed away in a car accident when he was three years old, and his mom raised him by herself, pulling double shifts at the hospital to try and make ends meet. As soon as Sam was old enough to work, he got a job and helped his mom with the bills.

"Cal was a friend of my dad's and when I was about thirteen years old, he started teaching me how to fix cars. When I turned sixteen, he hired me to help him at his garage."

I was in awe of this boy, who worked not only for himself, but also to help his mom pay her bills. I wanted to cry because I'd never met a person who thought more about others than themselves. I poured out my soul to him about my family and how I felt; maybe it was too soon, but I felt comfortable talking to Sam, and it just felt right. He held my hand as I told him about Corinne, Zoey, and Dylan. I saw his eyes turn dark gray when I told him what Dylan had tried last year. I assured him it was okay because I'd threatened him and he knew I would make good on those threats.

"Tell me you like Mexican fried ice cream," he said excitedly.

I looked down and, with a small smile, I said, "I don't like it; I love it!"

He went from disappointed to happy in a matter of a split second. The waiter brought our ice cream and gave us each a spoon. Sam swiftly ran his spoon through the whipped cream.

"Open up." He smiled as he held the spoon to my mouth.

My heart started pounding and the butterflies got all excited and started dancing around. I opened my mouth as he fed me the whipped cream. I knew it was only our first date, but I think I was starting to fall in love with him. It felt right. He felt right. Being with him felt right. After we finished off the ice cream, Sam paid the bill and took my hand. He led me out of the restaurant and to the small park that was across the street. It was a beautiful night and the stars brightly lit up the sky. We each took a seat on the swings and slowly swung back and forth as we continued to talk about our hopes and dreams.

Sam took me home after we spent an hour at the park because it was a school night. He pulled in my driveway, and I struggled because I didn't want this night to end. He reached over and gently traced the outline of my jaw with his finger.

"You are very beautiful, Claire Montgomery, and I had the best night of my life with you."

I stared into his blue-gray eyes and leaned closer into him, focusing on his lips. He gently put his mouth on mine and kissed me softly. I started to tremble. He cupped the back of my neck as he kissed me; his tongue opened my lips and slid softly into my mouth. I followed his lead and let my tongue join his. His mouth was amazing, and it set my body on fire. I desired him, all of him, from this one kiss. He let out a deep groan, which drove me wild as I ran my fingers through his brown hair. He moved his mouth from my lips to my neck and started kissing me softly by my ear. I panted as he moved his hand down to my breast and cupped it through my shirt. He stopped and pulled away.

"Claire, I'm sorry. We have to stop," he said, panting.

"You have nothing to be sorry for, Sam."

I wanted to tell him that I was a virgin. Even though I was embarrassed, I told him anyway because he had a right to know. He smiled at me and pushed my hair back off my shoulder.

"Good, that makes me happy that you've saved yourself for someone special."

I put my hand on his as he held my face. "Thank you."

He kissed my forehead and then the tip of my nose. "Since tomorrow is Friday. Will you consider going out with me again?"

I put my arms around his neck and hugged him tight. "I can't wait to see you again." We kissed goodnight and Sam walked me up to the door.

"See you tomorrow, Claire." He smiled as we both had a hard time letting go of each other's hand.

"See you tomorrow, Sam." I smiled back.

Harry and Corinne were sitting in the living room and both turned their heads when they heard the door open.

"Hi, Claire. How was your date?" Harry asked.

I walked over to where they were sitting. "It was amazing, Dad. I had the best time."

"It's good to see you smile."

"Does this boy go to college?" Corinne asked.

And there it was: the interrogation and questioning as if I was on trial. "No, Mom, he doesn't. He works full time so he can help his mom with the bills. His dad passed away when he was three years old and she raised him as a single mom."

Corinne rolled her eyes. "I don't think you should see him again. You can do so much better."

"Too bad," I spat. "We're going out tomorrow night."

Harry decided it was time to step in. "Claire, go to bed, and Corinne, just stop, please just stop."

She got up and huffed all the way to her bedroom. I said good night to Harry and headed up to my room. As soon as I changed into my pajamas, I climbed into bed and read a text that came from Sam.

"*I miss you already, Claire. Maybe it's too soon, but I really like you.*"

My heart melted as I responded back.

"*I miss you, Sam, and I really like you too. Goodnight.*"

"*Goodnight, babe.*"

I smiled as I read his last message and fell into a deep sleep.

# *Chapter 4*

The next morning, I awoke to a good morning text.

*"Have a good day at school and I'll see you later."*

*"Good morning. I'll have a great day as soon as I see you!"*

I was having Rachel drive me to the garage so I could pick up my car after school. The three of us sat at lunch and I was grilled about Sam and our date.

"You are in love, Claire Montgomery," Ally pointed out.

I just smiled and shrugged my shoulders. She was right, I think I was in love. As soon as the last bell rang, we hopped into Rachel's car and headed to Irvine to pick up my car.

"Thanks for taking me," I said.

"No problem, friend; that's what I'm here for." Rachel smiled.

We pulled up to the garage and I saw Sam standing there, talking to Cal. The minute I saw him, my stomach went into a craze and my heart started racing. He looked over at me and smiled as I got out of the car. He waved to Rachel before she drove off, and I walked over to him and Cal with a smile on my face.

"Hey, Cal. How are you?"

"Doing well, Claire. It's good to see you again." He smiled as he walked away.

Sam reached over, grabbed my waist, and pulled me closer to him, gently kissing my lips.

"Hi," he whispered.

"Hi," I whispered back.

He handed me the keys and told me not to worry, that the car was taken care of.

"How much do I owe you, Sam?"

He softly kissed my lips again. "A date, that's all."

"Please let me pay you for the repairs."

He shook his head no and opened my car door. "Mark my words, Sam Snow, I will repay you."

He smiled as he gave me a soft kiss. "See you tonight, Claire," he said as he shut the door.

I drove home, listening to Coldplay and smiling as I thought about Sam. As soon as I walked through the door, I was summoned to the kitchen.

"Claire, I need you to come to dinner with us tonight. We are going with Dylan and his family to discuss the engagement party."

"Mom, no, I'm going out with Sam tonight and you knew that."

"It's not open for discussion. You're going."

"I'm not going, and I don't care what you say. I already made plans, and I'm not cancelling them."

Zoey got up from the table. "Mom, just forget it. If she wants to go out with the grease monkey, then let her. I don't want her at dinner anyway."

The furnace inside me lit up and my skin started to burn; nobody called Sam a grease monkey and got away with it. I balled my left fist and, before I knew it, I pushed Zoey to the ground and socked her right in the cheek. Corinne ran over and grabbed me off of her.

"What the hell is the matter with you, Claire? Oh my God."

"I'm sick of her, and I'm sick of you always taking her side." I looked down at Zoey, who was holding her cheek and crying. "And, as for you, don't you ever call Sam a grease monkey again, you stupid skanky bitch."

I tore through the kitchen and up the stairs to my room, slamming the door. Oh boy, was I in trouble now, but I didn't care. It felt good to punch Zoey and tell her off. Only a few more months of this hell and I was off to college, and I didn't plan on ever coming back. I sat on my bed, waiting for Hurricane Corinne to blow through, but she never did.

A while later, Harry came knocking on my door, asking if he could come in. I opened the door for him and waved him in.

"Corinne sent you to do her dirty work?" I asked.

"No. Your mother is very upset. What you did to Zoey, I didn't think you had it in you." He smiled.

He sat on the edge of my bed and patted it for me to sit down. "Claire, I get how much this boy means to you. I can see it on your face and in your eyes, and what your mother and sister are doing is wrong, and I will talk to them, but I need you to do something for me."

I looked at the pain in his eyes. "What do you need me to do?"

"I need you to go and apologize to your sister and mother."

I quickly stood up. "You want me to apologize for them calling the boy I like a grease monkey? Are you kidding me, Dad?"

"Claire, you are the better person and you know it. Please, just do it for me," he begged.

I took in a deep breath and clenched my jaw. "Fine, I'll apologize, but let me tell you something, I wish I was never born into this family. I love you, Dad, but when I leave for college, I'm never coming back."

"Don't say that, Claire. You're upset right now."

I threw open the door and went to Corinne's room, where she was putting ice on Zoey's cheek. "I'm sorry I hit you, Zoey. It was wrong and I will never do it again."

"Get out of here!" she screamed.

I walked out and shut the door. The bruise on her cheek was noticeable. Oh well, she deserved it.

****

As soon as I saw Sam's car coming up the drive, I ran outside and waited for him to pull up. I didn't even give him a chance to get out and open the door for me. I instantly climbed in and hugged him.

"Hey, what's wrong?"

"I'm just happy to see you."

"I'm happy to see you too." He smiled and then drove down the driveway.

I told him what happened with Zoey, but I didn't tell him what she said.

"Remind me never to piss you off." He chuckled.

We drove to the beach and Sam pulled a picnic basket from the back seat. He opened my door and took my hand to help me out.

"I thought we could have dinner while watching the sunset."

Tears started to sting my eyes, for no one had ever done something so special for me before. He took my hand and we walked down towards the water. We found a spot that we liked and I helped him set a large blanket down on the sand. I sat down on the blanket and watched as the waves lapped to the shore. The air was warm and there wasn't a trace of wind. It was the perfect night to watch the sunset in Newport Beach. Sam opened the basket and pulled out several submarine sandwiches, five different bags of chips, and four bottles of Coke.

"Wow, are you planning on feeding an army?"

"I wasn't sure what kind of sandwiches you liked, so I got a variety; same with the chips."

I smiled at him and sighed. I grabbed his shirt and pulled him towards me as I softly kissed his lips.

"What's that for?" Sam smiled.

I grinned as I gently nipped his bottom lip. "Just for being you and nothing more."

He wrapped his arms around me and held me tight. We sat on the blanket, ate our subs and chips, and drank our Coke while we talked about life. After we finished eating, Sam laid down and pulled me close to him, so that I was lying in his arms. We watched the sunset over the ocean. It was beautiful, but not as beautiful as that moment that I was lying wrapped up in him. We looked at each other as our lips met and our tongues started to tango. He rolled so he was hovering over me, his beautiful eyes staring into mine, as if he wanted to devour me. He started to kiss my neck, and as I started to moan, he moved to my lips. My hands moved up and down his back as I pulled him in tighter, feeling his erection. His hands rubbed up and down my hips and slowly moved to my breasts. He let out low groans that made me want more of him. My insides started burning with desire and the ache below was on fire.

"Sam, I want you to make love to me."

He stopped and looked at me. "Claire, are you sure? You need to be sure; it's a big step."

"I'm positive. I've never wanted anything more in my life. I saved myself for *you*, I know that."

He smiled and kissed me again. "I don't want your first time to be here; you need to be comfortable. My mom is working a double tonight, so we can go to my house."

We got up, packed up the basket and blanket, and drove to his house in Santa Ana. Was it too soon to have sex since I'd only known him a few days? In most cases, yes, and I never would have slept with a guy on the second date. But with Sam, it was different. He was different because when I was with him, I felt like I'd known him forever. We connected in ways and on levels that I never could've imagined. We were born for each other.

****

His house was small, only two bedrooms, but cute and comfortable. The outside was beige vinyl siding with white trim and, off to the side, his mom had planted an array of flowers. It was very pretty and it felt like a home. Not a status place where you invite friends over to show off your money, and certainly not a home where you compete with other elites to have the bigger and better home. We stepped inside the house and Sam flicked the light switch. The house was immaculate. It consisted of a small living room with a couch, chair, and TV, a kitchen with a small round table with two chairs, a bathroom, and two bedrooms. Sam took my hand and kissed my knuckles where bruises were left from Zoey's face.

He led me to his bedroom and shut the door. He slowly took off his shirt and unbuttoned his pants. He walked towards me and kissed me softly while stroking my hair.

"I promise to be careful and not hurt you," he whispered. "If you're uncomfortable and want to stop, we will. I want this to be a great experience for you."

"Thank you. But don't worry about me, I'll be fine."

He pulled my shirt over my head and moved his hands over my bra. He kissed me softly, starting from my ear and down my neck to my throat. I groaned and threw my head back. He took his fingers and slowly undid my bra, letting it fall to the floor as he unbuttoned my jeans and proceeded to take them down. He laid me gently on the bed and, as he took off his pants, he stared at me the entire time.

"You are so beautiful, Claire. I hope you know that. I've never wanted anyone like I want you."

He took my erect nipple in his mouth, sucking and lightly tugging at each one. I groaned as I could feel the warmth and the twinges in between my thighs. I arched my lower back so my hips dug into him. He moved his hands down the front of my panties and felt the wetness that emerged from his pleasure. He stared at me as he slowly inserted his finger inside me, moving it in and out. I moaned and brought his head down so I could kiss him. I took my hand and moved it over his underwear, feeling his erection and sliding my hand down the front, feeling his hardness in my bare hands. I stroked it up and down lightly. He groaned and moaned, which made his fingers move in and out of me faster. I felt strange, like I was going to explode.

"You're so wet and tight, Claire. Are you ready for me?" he asked as he reached in his nightstand drawer and pulled out a condom.

He took a hold of his penis and covered it with the condom, then he gently placed it in between my legs and slowly pushed inside of me. I moaned loudly.

"Are you okay?" he asked.

I looked at his face and ran my hands through his hair.

"I'm great," I said as one single, happy tear fell from my eye.

He pushed deeper until he was fully inside me, thrusting in and out slowly. I could feel myself building up, my body needing to release itself. I started to moan. "Faster, Sam, go faster." He kissed me as he moved in and out of me, faster and faster, causing me and him to come at the same time. He yelled my name as I did his and dug my nails down his back. Sam collapsed on top of me and hugged me. He whispered something in my ear that I will never forget. "I think I'm falling in love with you, Claire."

I think he was stunned he said it. He looked up at me and said he was sorry. I ran my finger down his cheek. "Don't be sorry. I know how you feel. I think I'm falling in love with you too."

Sam smiled and after he climbed back in bed from disposing the condom, I lay in his arms and we talked about our feelings for each other. Even though we had only known each other for a few days, it felt like a lifetime and the feeling was for both us. I believe everyone has a soul mate and Sam was mine, and I was his. I wanted to stay with him all night, but I knew tonight was not the night because of what had happened with Corinne and Zoey. He drove me home and, as bad as it hurt to say our goodbyes, we did.

"Later, baby." He smiled as he ran his finger down my cheek.

"Later, baby," I replied with a kiss.

I put my key in the door, walked up the stairs, and took a hot shower. I climbed in my bed wishing he were lying next to me.

# *Chapter 5*

I woke up the next morning to two missed texts from Ally and Rachel, demanding to know how my night with Sam went. I got up, dressed, and mustered up enough nerve to join the family for Saturday breakfast. I walked downstairs to the smell of pancakes, eggs, and bacon.

"Smells good in here," I said.

Harry and Zoey were sitting at the table and Corinne was cooking.

"There's our girl." Harry smiled.

"Good morning, Claire." Corinne spoke only because she had to.

I poured a cup of coffee and sat at the table. Zoey looked up at me and, oh, her nasty little bruise was worse today. I really left my mark. I silently smiled.

"Zoey, I'm really sorry," I said as I tried so hard not to laugh.

"Save it, sis. I don't want your apology. You're a disgrace."

"Zoey, that's enough," Harry yelled.

I put my hand on his arm. "It's okay, Dad. She has every right to hate me. What I did was wrong and I'm sorry, but I know, in time, she'll forgive me."

I got up from the table, grabbed my coffee, and went up to my room. I called Ally and Rachel and asked them to come over so we could talk before I saw Sam. About thirty minutes later, I heard voices coming up the stairs and I knew it was them. My bedroom door flew open and the two of them ran into my room and jumped on the bed.

"Spill, Claire. We need details now," Rachel said.

I smiled as I got up from the bed and walked to the closet to find the perfect outfit.

"It was amazing and the most beautiful experience of my life. He was so gentle, so he didn't hurt me and he kept asking me if I was okay."

Ally squealed. "He's perfect. Oh my God, I want a man like him."

"Claire, what are you going to do?" Rachel asked.

I turned around and looked at her in confusion. "Do about what?"

"Your parents. You know Corinne and Harry won't approve and Corinne is known to cause problems."

"I'm not worried about Corinne. I can handle her. All I have to do is make it through these next few months and then I'm out of here and away from her. She will not control my life anymore."

"Oh, by the way, good job on Zoey. We saw her when we walked in." Ally smiled. "I knew that would happen one of these days."

I laughed as I pulled a sundress from the closet and got ready for my day with Sam.

\*\*\*\*

I drove out to Sam's house this time so I could meet his mom. When I pulled up to his house, she was just getting home from work. She turned to me as she shut the car door.

"Hi, Ms. Snow, I'm Claire." I smiled.

She had the same smile as Sam. "Hi, Claire, it's so nice to meet you. Please come inside."

I followed her in the house and Sam was making a fresh pot of coffee. He walked over to me and he kissed and hugged me like he hadn't seen me in months.

"I see you two met."

"Yes, and she's a very lovely girl, Sam."

Sam's mom was an attractive woman. She stood about five feet, five inches tall with a small frame and blonde hair that was cut into a bob. I was surprised she never married again after Sam's father passed away. She was on her way to bed and we were heading out the door.

"It was great to meet you, Mrs. Snow."

"The pleasure was all mine, Claire." She smiled as she kissed me on the cheek.

Sam and I had a great day; we bowled, had lunch on a patio outside a small Italian restaurant, took a walk along the beach, and just enjoyed each other's company. I loved hearing about his childhood and how he grew up. The stories he told about him and his mom after his father passed away were touching. The closeness and the bond he had with his mom was something I wished I could have with Corinne, but she'd always see me as different.

As we continued our walk along the beach, I had something I wanted to ask Sam. "My sister's engagement party is next month, and I would like it if you would come."

"I don't think your parents would want me there, Claire. We both know what your mom thinks of me."

"You let me handle Corinne; I want you there by my side so I can show you off to everyone."

He smiled and gently kissed me on the lips. "If it will make you happy, then fine, I'll come."

"Do you own a suit?" I asked with a smile.

Sam laughed and grabbed the tip of my nose. "Yes, I own a suit, smarty pants."

I went home early that night because Sam had to be at the garage at the crack of dawn. I walked through the door, only to find Harry, Corinne, Zoey, and Dylan all sitting in the living room having drinks and laughing. That was something I would never have with my family and Sam. Dylan looked my way and gave me the dirtiest of looks for what I did to Zoey. I couldn't help but smirk at him.

"You're home early," Corinne said.

"Sam has to work in the morning. Hey, I invited him to the engagement party."

Corinne whipped her head around so fast I thought she was going to get whiplash. "You what?" she snapped.

"Corinne, calm down," Harry said.

"I will not have that…"

I balled my left fist this time so Zoey could see it. "Whatever, Claire. Invite your boyfriend and embarrass yourself."

"Claire, we will talk about this later," Corinne said.

"If Sam is not welcome, then I'm not either," I snapped and ran up the stairs.

When I reached my bedroom, I texted Sam and told him how much I loved him and that I missed him. There was no way Corinne was going to stop me from seeing him.

A few seconds later, he replied.

*"I love you, Claire. Have sweet dreams and we'll be together tomorrow."*

I smiled and my heart melted a little more. I was totally in love with this boy and nobody could tell me any different.

# *Chapter 6*

Sam and I were inseparable. We'd been dating for almost two months now and we saw each other every day, even if it was for a couple of hours. Corinne was barely talking to me these days and Zoey wouldn't even look at me. Not only were they pissed because I gave Dylan's ticket to Sam for my graduation, she was still pissed about that punch I threw at her. Not to mention the fact that I refused a production of a graduation party Corinne had spent years planning. I only wanted a simple dinner with Sam and his mom. Unfortunately, my family had to join us.

It was around eleven a.m. and, as I just finished getting dressed, my phone rang and it was Sam.

"Hi, babe," I answered.

"I have a surprise for you today. Are you ready to go?"

"Go where?" I asked.

"Just tell me if you're dressed."

"Of course I'm dressed."

I heard the doorbell ring. "Sam, hold on; someone's at the door."

I walked down the stairs and opened the door, only to see Sam standing there holding his phone to his ear. I smiled.

"Let me call you back. There's this really hot guy at my door smiling at me. Later, baby."

He hung up his phone and wrapped his arms around me, hugging me and making me feel safe.

"What's this about a surprise?" I asked.

"You'll see. Let's get out of here and grab some lunch."

Corinne was walking by and stopped dead in her tracks.

"Hi, Mrs. Montgomery," Sam smiled.

"Hello Sam," she managed and then continued to walk towards the living room.

"Wow, that was awkward," he said.

"She's an ice queen; just ignore her." I smiled.

Sam and I jumped into his car and drove to a little sandwich shop on Bristol Street. He ordered our sandwiches and we ate outside on the patio.

"Sam, the suspense is killing me. What's this surprise you were talking about?"

He looked at me and laughed. "You're as bad a kid before Christmas."

He pulled out a white envelope from his pocket and handed it to me. "Read this."

I took it from his hand and opened the letter inside. It read:

*"Dear Mr. Snow, on behalf of the staff here at the University of Washington, it is our pleasure to announce the acceptance of your application to our university this fall."*

I looked at Sam and he was smiling at me.

"Does this mean? I mean are you—?" I couldn't spit out the words. Excitement took over my entire body and I began to shake.

"Yes, yes! I'm going with you to the University of Washington."

I jumped out of my seat and jumped onto his lap, hugging him tight and kissing his lips.

"When did you do this? How did you do this? Why? Oh my God, Sam, we don't have to say goodbye."

"I applied a few weeks ago, and I did it for us, so we can be together. I've wanted to go to college, but I felt like I couldn't because I had to take care of my mom. I sat down and talked to her and she cried and told me how she wanted nothing more than for me to go. Cal said he would keep an eye on her."

Tears started to fall down my face. Sam took his thumb and softly wiped them away. "Don't cry, Claire."

"I'm so happy. I can't help it."

After hugging and kissing him for a few more moments, I got off his lap and sat down back in my chair to finish eating my sandwich. There was an older couple sitting at the table next to us. As they got up to leave, the older woman looked at us.

"Young love is a rarity these days, but I can tell you two have it." She winked.

We both smiled as they left the patio. I was so happy and nothing was going to ruin it. I wasn't going to tell Harry and Corinne that Sam was going to the University of Washington with me. It was none of their business because, once I left home, I wasn't coming back. Everything I was worried about was now fading away and life seemed perfect. Now all I had to do was get the hell away from my family.

\*\*\*\*

Sam dropped me off at home while he and his mom went shopping. He asked me to come with him and, as much as I wanted to, I felt it was important for him to spend some time alone with her since they didn't see each other very much, especially now that he was going away to college. I walked into the kitchen and found Corinne sitting at the table with Dylan and Zoey. She glanced my way and asked me to please sit down. There was something she needed to talk to me about. My stomach tied itself in knots; when Corinne tells you to sit down it was never good news. I didn't feel comfortable sitting at the table by Dylan, and whatever Corinne had to say, it was not going to be in front of him.

"Whatever you need to say, Mom, can we please do it in private and not in front of an audience?"

"Claire, please. Can you for once in your life listen to me?"

I rolled my eyes and glared over at Zoey and Dylan, who were staring at me with excitement in their eyes. Whatever Corinne had to tell me, I got the feeling those two were behind it. I leaned my elbows on the island and crossed my legs. "Spit it out, Mom. I'm listening."

Corinne shifted in her chair. "Did you know that Sam has an arrest record?"

I twisted my face at her. "Okay, and?"

"Did you know, Claire?" she asked with persistence.

"No, Mom, I didn't," I snapped.

"This boy, you claim to know so well, had an arrest record for dealing drugs."

"That was the past; he doesn't do or deal drugs. What the hell is this about, anyway, and how do you know this?" I looked over at Dylan, who instantly looked away.

I pointed my finger at him. "You, you had something to do with this, didn't you?" I yelled as I started walking towards him. He put both hands up.

"Claire, stop!" Corinne yelled.

"I asked Dylan if he could do some checking for me because I wanted to know what kind of boy you were seeing."

My face turned red and my heart started racing. *How dare she,* was all I thought.

"The boy has a criminal record, Claire, and he didn't even tell you."

I put both hands over my ears and turned for the stairs.

"You are not to see that boy anymore!" Corrine yelled as she followed me up the stairs.

"Mom, stop! You don't even know him!"

"I know enough not to like him." She chased after me.

I stepped in my bedroom and turned towards the door. "You don't like him because he's not rich and he doesn't live in a big fancy house," I snapped.

Corrine followed me into my room. "He's not good enough for you and I don't want you seeing him."

"Really, Mother? Are you worried that I'll tarnish your reputation, give your friends something to talk about, or better yet, that I'll disgrace the Montgomery name?"

"Claire, that's not fair."

"Not fair?" I yelled. "What's not fair is you judging Sam for where he comes from instead of getting to know him as a person."

"This discussion is over and so is your relationship," she said as she turned on her heels and stomped out of my room.

Tears started to sting my eyes as I lay on my bed, looking at the picture of us on my phone. Sam was perfect to me and I loved him. I just wished I could make my mother and father see that. The tears rolled down my face like someone opened the floodgates. I wasn't crying for what Corinne told me about Sam; I was crying because of what she did, and how she did it. I needed a plan. I couldn't stay here anymore, and I would never look at Corinne or Zoey the same way again. And then there was Dylan, stupid boy. I hoped he realized he just dug his own grave. I grabbed my suitcase from my closet and started throwing some clothes in it. I reached for a shoebox that was hidden in the corner on the top shelf and grabbed the money I had been saving and shoved it in my purse. I dialed Sam.

"Hey, babe, what's up?" The sound of his voice calmed me.

"Sam, I need you to come get me. I'm leaving home, and I need you, please." I started crying again.

"Claire, what happened?" he asked with worry.

"I'll explain everything when you get here, but don't come up the drive. I'll meet you at the end. Just text me when you're here."

"I'm on my way, sweetheart. I love you."

"I love you too. Please hurry." I hung up and packed a few more items.

I grabbed a pink duffel bag from under my bed and filled it with all my girly things, such as makeup and hair products. Before long, my phone chimed with a text from Sam.

*"Here, baby."*

I quietly opened my door and peeked from side to side, making sure no one was there. I quietly tiptoed down the stairs, being careful not to make a sound. When I reached the bottom, I could hear Corinne talking from the kitchen. I slowly opened the front door and stepped outside. Mission accomplished; I was out and no one had heard me. I ran down the drive to Sam's car. He got out immediately, grabbed my bags, and threw them in the trunk. I got into the car and told him to go and get out of here before someone saw us. As Sam pulled away, a feeling of exhilaration came over me. I threw my head back and let out a deep breath.

"Are you okay? What happened in there?" Sam asked as he grabbed my hand and held it tight.

I couldn't bring myself to tell him what Corinne had said. It didn't matter to me anyway, so I had to come up with something quickly. This was going to be the first lie I ever told him.

"It was just the last straw, Sam. Corinne started in on me in front of Zoey and Dylan about the engagement party, and I just couldn't take anymore."

He let go of my hand and gently wiped away a tear that fell from my eye.

"I don't want to talk about it anymore. I'm out of there and that's all that matters."

"It's okay, baby, you don't have to talk about it. You're going to stay at my house." He smiled.

I looked over at his sweet face and smiled. "Are you sure your mom won't mind?"

"No. I already talked to her about it. My mom loves you and said you can move in. Besides, she would love to have another female around the house."

He stopped at the red light, and I leaned over to kiss his cheek. "Thank you," I whispered.

Sam kissed the top of my head and the light turned green. He stepped on the gas pedal and, halfway through the light, I saw two sets of headlights coming at us. I screamed for Sam to stop as I heard a loud crash and everything went black.

## *Chapter 7*

I could hear the beeping sounds of a monitor. I looked around and saw myself lying in a hospital bed, hooked up to a monitor and ventilator. I didn't recognize myself, for my head was wrapped up in white bandages and there were multiple contusions on my face. *Was I dead? How could I stand here and look at my own body?*

Corinne was kneeling at my bedside, holding my hand and crying. I felt somewhat sorry for her. Harry was pacing back and forth across the room, running his hands through his hair. The pained look on his face tore me apart. *How did I get here? What happened?* Suddenly, the room door opened and a man in a white coat entered.

"Mr. and Mrs. Montgomery, Claire has suffered severe trauma to her head. We had to go in and stop the bleeding on her brain."

Corinne grabbed onto Harry as if she was going to pass out.

"Claire's brain is severely swollen right now and we had to put her in a medically induced coma until the swelling subsides. We needed to remove her spleen and stop the internal bleeding. Her ribs are shattered and her left arm is broken. To be honest with you, Mr. and Mrs. Montgomery, it's a miracle your daughter is alive."

Harry could barely speak. "What are Claire's chances, doctor?"

The doctor answered, "We aren't sure at this point. The next forty-eight to seventy-two hours are the most critical. I'm sorry, but that's all I can give you for now."

The doctor walked out of the room, and Corinne and Harry cried in each other's arms. I walked over to where I was lying on the bed and stared at myself. I needed to find Sam. Where was he? I needed to make sure he was okay. If anything happened to him, I would let go because there would be no place in this world for me without him. I walked out of my room and heard the crying sounds of a woman down the hall. I followed the sound that led me to Sam's room. I stood there and stared at the love of my life, who lay there helplessly, hooked up to the same monitor and ventilator as I was. His head was wrapped in white bandages and his face was so swollen, I barely recognized him. I walked over to his mom, who was holding his hand to her face as she cried and begged him to wake up. I reached out to touch her, but my hand went right through her. I looked at my hand in confusion. *What the hell was happening?* I leaned down close to Sam's face and whispered to him.

"You have to wake up, Sam. I need you."

As I went to kiss his head, I found that I couldn't. I couldn't touch him. I was startled and, as I turned to run back to my room, I found myself standing in the middle of the most beautiful garden. The sun was shining down on me, filling my skin and body with warmth. I could smell the fragrance from each flower in the garden; it was the most beautiful smell I have ever encountered. I looked around for someone or something. I felt so much love and peace here that I didn't want to leave.

"Claire," I heard a voice whisper. I turned my head in the direction it came from, but no one was there. When I turned back around, I saw a woman dressed in white standing barefoot across the garden from me. She was thin and pale; her hair was pure white and fell down to her waist.

"Claire, it's not your time. You cannot stay here," she spoke softly.

"I don't want to leave."

The woman smiled. "I know you don't, but you have to. The road to recovery will be hard, but you will get through it, I promise."

"Sam, where is Sam?" I asked.

"Your beloved is not here, Claire. His road to recovery will be long and hard as well. If your love was true and eternal, you will find each other again."

She started to fade, and it felt like someone was pulling me away. "Wait! What do you mean by that?" I screamed as I held out my hand to reach her. I was fighting to stay in the garden, but the force that was pulling me back was much stronger.

I opened my eyes and looked around the room. My head was pounding and everything was blurry. The slow and steady beeping sound of the monitor was not helping. A girl that was sitting in the chair next to my bed jumped up and screamed, "Mom, wake up! Claire's awake!"

The woman on the other side of the bed lifted her head and started crying.

"My baby. You came back to us."

The girl ran out of the room, yelling for the doctor. The doctor came into the room with the nurse and both of them walked over to me.

"Good afternoon. I'm Dr. Georgeson. Can you tell me your name?"

I looked at him and blinked a few times, then I looked at the nurse, who was smiling at me.

"Can you tell me your name?" he asked once more.

I looked at him and whispered, "I think my name is Claire."

The woman broke down and started crying as the girl held her. The doctor took out his little flashlight and shined it in both my eyes.

"Do you remember what happened to you?" he asked.

I was assuming there was an accident since I was all bandaged up and lying in a hospital bed. "Accident?" I whispered.

"That's right; you were in a very bad car accident. It's a miracle you're here with us."

The woman grabbed my hand. "Welcome back, Claire," she cried.

The doctor continued to examine me. "Claire, do you know what year it is?"

I had no clue.

"Do you know where you live?"

I had no clue.

"Do you know how old you are?"

I whispered, "I'm not sure."

"Eighteen, baby, you're eighteen now," Corinne cried.

The doctor continued. "Do you remember these people, Claire?"

I nodded my head. "Mom and sister."

"Good. That's right." He smiled. "Mrs. Montgomery, Claire has amnesia due to the head trauma she suffered from the accident. She can remember very little about her life right now."

"How long will this last? When will she start remembering things?" she asked.

"I don't know. It's hard to tell. It could take a few days, a few months, a few years or there is the possibility that she may never regain her full memory back," he said. "Make her comfortable and try to help her remember. Her recovery will be long and painful, and she will need your support," he said as he turned and walked out of the room.

****

I spent six weeks lying in a hospital bed and recovering. My mom spent every day with me and my dad came and stayed with me after he got off from work. My friends Rachel and Ally came by to see me on the last day before I was discharged. They visited me frequently, and even though I didn't quite remember who they were, they seemed really nice. I sat in a wheelchair as Rachel pushed me down the hallway and out to the courtyard. It was a beautiful summer day as the sun was shining, and the birds were softly chirping. I stayed in my wheelchair as my friends sat down on the bench.

"I brought you some lunch." Ally smiled as she handed me a little brown wicker basket with a cloth napkin covering the top. I smiled back and removed the napkin.

"It's the lunches we used to eat at school," Rachel said.

Tucked inside the basket was a turkey sandwich with cheese and lettuce on wheat, a bag of baked Lays potato chips, a can of Coke, and a chocolate chip cookie.

"Thank you. It looks great."

"I thought maybe it would trigger some memories," Ally said.

Rachel took out her phone. "I want to show you some pictures. Maybe it will help you remember."

I looked at her and then down at her phone. She had so many pictures of the three of us at school, at a dance, and in a bedroom that I assumed was mine, but I wasn't sure.

"Here; you can scroll through them yourself," she said as she handed me her phone.

I dragged my finger along her screen, hoping that one of these pictures would trigger a memory. I stopped at a picture of me and some guy. A black flash went off in my mind, followed by a bright light. I jumped and the phone fell into my lap.

"Claire, what is it?"

I didn't know what had just happened, but it hurt. I picked up the phone from my lap and showed them the picture.

"Who am I with?"

They turned and looked at each other, and I could tell something was up.

"Umm, that's my cousin, Riley," Ally said as she took the phone out of my hand.

I cocked my head to the side. "Were we a couple or something? It looks like we were."

Rachel lightly tapped my arm. "Don't be silly. You two were good friends, and besides, he's gay."

Something didn't sit right with their answers. If we were such good friends, then why didn't he come visit me in the hospital? I felt something that I couldn't explain when I saw that picture.

## *Chapter 8*

Being home was strange. I didn't remember my room, but I loved how it was decorated in black and pink. I guess those were my favorite colors. I really couldn't tell you. Weeks went by, and still no recollection of my life. I was trying to make peace with the fact that I was starting my life over, because my old life had disappeared into a deep, black hole. I fell into a depression that left my mother and father worried about me. I asked my mom, over and over again, to tell me about the accident, but she wouldn't tell me and I could tell she was holding something back.

"It was a terrible and unfortunate accident, and it wasn't your fault. You need to stop dwelling on it and move on, Claire."

She told me I had been driving and that I was alone; if only I could remember where I was going that night. I felt like a puzzle and there were a ton of pieces missing. I asked my mom if she had my old cell phone, but she said it had been smashed in the accident, so they got me a new one.

My mother finally made an appointment for me to see Dr. Blakely. She was a psychologist who specialized in amnesia victims. She was worried about me and the depression I had gone into and my refusal to leave the house. She didn't understand what it was like to feel like a stranger in the only home I supposedly ever lived in. Even though I remembered her, Harry, and Zoey, there was nothing else about my life that I could call my own. I was a stranger in Claire Montgomery's body.

"Claire Montgomery," Dr. Blakely called into the waiting room.

I got up from my seat and followed her into her office. She asked me to please take a seat on the couch and make myself comfortable while she sat in the leather chair across from me. I was envious of her long, black straight hair. Her eyes were brown and her skin was sun kissed like she had just gotten back from vacation.

"How are you, Claire?" she asked kindly.

I fumbled with my hands and looked down. "I'm okay, I guess."

"Tell me what you remember about your life."

I started twisting my hair around my finger. "I don't remember anyone or anything except my mom, dad, and sister."

"Hmm," she said as she jotted something down on her pad of paper.

We sat and talked for the hour, and when the session was over, we scheduled another appointment. I liked Dr. Blakely; she was kind and easy to talk to. She recommended that I come see her at least twice a week and, when she felt I was ready, she was going to use hypnotherapy to see if it would trigger any memories. She prescribed an anti-depressant for me to help with the depression, but I didn't take them. Since my mother was watching every move I made, I took a pill out of the bottle every morning and flushed it down the toilet so there was always one less when she counted them.

****

Four more weeks passed, and today was the day that Dr. Blakely was going to use hypnotherapy on me. She instructed me to lie down on the couch and completely relax. She put a warm blanket over me and told me to picture in my mind where I'd like to go. She talked in a low voice and asked me if I was where I wanted to be.

"Yes," I answered.

"Good, Claire. Now I want you to go back to when you were five years old. What do you see?"

"I'm at my birthday party with my family and friends in our backyard. There were a lot of people there and I rode a pony and had a beautiful doll cake."

"Claire, I want you to fast forward to when you were thirteen."

"I'm with Ally and Rachel and we are at a park, rollerblading. Ouch, I fell and scraped my knee." I started to cry.

"Claire, I want you to go forward and stop at the age of seventeen."

All of a sudden, my mind started flashing through memories like a photo album; images of me and a boy dancing, holding hands, having fun, kissing, touching and being together. My body was overcome with happiness and I felt whole. Then, suddenly, I was in a car and all I saw were headlights blinding my eyes.

"Sam!" I started screaming.

"Claire, I'm going to count to 5 and you are to wake up. 1.2.3.4.5. Snap."

I awoke instantly and found myself covered in sweat. I looked at Dr. Blakely as I swallowed hard.

"Claire, who is Sam?"

I looked at her and then looked around the room. "I don't know."

She scribbled down something on her pad and the session was over. I walked out of her office feeling worse than I had in months. It seemed like all the progress I made vanished, just like my memories. I never went back after that day.

I couldn't stop thinking about the name Sam. When I got home, I went right to the kitchen where Corinne was helping with dinner.

"How was your appointment, Claire?" she asked.

"Mom, did I know someone named Sam?"

She stopped stirring the sauce and froze for a moment. She turned around and looked at me.

"Samantha was one of your girlfriends."

"Was she in the car with me?"

"Why are you asking this and how did you remember that name?"

"Dr. Blakely used hypnotherapy on me today and I screamed the name Sam."

I could tell she was uncomfortable. She asked me to sit down at the table with her. She took a hold of my hands and gently squeezed them.

"Sam died in the accident."

Tears started to fall from my eyes. "What?"

"We didn't want to tell you because we didn't want you to blame yourself. It wasn't your fault, Claire. She was sitting in the passenger's seat."

I couldn't control the tears as my mother reached over and hugged me. "It's okay, sweetie. It's time for you to move on from that horrible accident."

"But, my friend died!"

"It wasn't your fault and don't you dare blame yourself."

"What about her family? I have to talk to them!" I exclaimed.

"You can't, Claire. After the accident, they moved away. This is why we didn't want to tell you."

I pretended to be okay, just so Corinne would stop talking. I couldn't believe that someone died while I was driving. They said it wasn't my fault, but I still felt like it was. I wanted something in remembrance of Sam, but there weren't any pictures or anything around. I called Ally and Rachel and they confirmed Corinne's story. They said they would try to dig up some pictures of her, but they never did. After a while, and getting the feeling that I was being lied to, I gave up trying to talk to Corinne and Harry about the accident. I had a feeling there was way more than what they were telling me. In due time, I would make it my mission to find out what they were hiding.

****

I spent my time learning things I didn't know before the accident. I learned to play the piano and guitar fluently. My mother said I had a natural talent for music. I would sit at the piano and play for hours, drowning my sadness in the piano keys and creating my own sad melodies. I walked around the neighborhood, the park, and even the town, hoping the littlest sight would jog a memory. I went to the beach and walked along the shore. I set down a blanket and sat down with my knees to my chest. I stared out into the blue ocean water and watched the waves lap against the shore. I felt like I was drawn here, that I was supposed to be here. I couldn't explain the feeling or why; all I knew was that I needed to be at the beach. I sat there on my blanket with the warm soft sand underneath me while the sun was getting ready to set. Suddenly, my head started to hurt, and as I clutched the sides with my hands, I saw a flashback of a beach with me and someone sitting on a blanket. I was laughing. Instantly, bright lights were blinding me, and I heard the loud sound of a crash. My mind finally settled and the images were gone. The only thing I was left with was a headache. I folded up the blanket and headed home. Dr. Blakely had prescribed me some medication in case my headaches got worse. I opened my medicine cabinet and pulled out the bottle. I fumbled with the white childproof cap and shook one pill into my hand. I took it with a glass of water and went to bed.

# *Chapter 9*

It had been three years since the accident and nothing more than a few flashing lights and shadowy images filled my mind. Memories were far and gone except for the new ones I made when I awoke from my coma. I went on with my life the best I could. Zoey had married Dylan a year before and they were expecting their first baby. My mom and Zoey tried occasionally to set me up on dates, but the truth was I wasn't interested in dating, and I wasn't interested in relationships. I felt like half a person and it wasn't fair to the poor guy only to get half of me. Besides, I never connected with anyone. My heart ached and I had no explanation for it. Even after three years, there wasn't a day that went by that my heart wasn't hurting. I'd given up trying to figure out my life before the accident, which was enough to drive any sane person right into the loony bin. I couldn't stay sheltered in my past life or in this house anymore. I needed to start fresh, somewhere new and on my own. My parents sued the driver of the other car and put the settlement in my bank account. I didn't care about the money at the time, but now that I was planning to leave, it would come in handy. The first thing I needed to do was to pick a city where I wanted to start my new life. I got on my laptop and pulled up a map of the United States. I looked at New York City, Chicago, and Las Vegas, but they weren't appealing to me, at least not to live. My pop-up blocker must have been turned off because a pop up for Seattle's Best Coffee came across my computer. I stared at the word "Seattle." I must have wanted to go there because I was set to attend the University of Washington before the accident according to Corinne. That was it; Seattle was the city I would start my new life in. I typed Expedia.com into the address bar and searched flights from Newport Beach to Seattle. The next flight out was tomorrow morning at seven. I called a cab to be at my house at four.

I sat down at my desk and wrote a letter to my family:

*Dear Mom and Dad,*

*I want to thank you for everything you have done for me. As you are reading this, I will be on my way somewhere new to start my life on my own. I'm not sure where I'm going, but I will call you when I get settled. This is something I have to do for me, and I hope you can understand that. I don't really know what I'm looking for, but I know it's not here in Newport Beach. I will be forever grateful for all your support. I love you both very much, so please don't cry, and let me go do what I need to find myself.*

*Love,*

*Your daughter, Claire.*

I felt horrible for not telling them where I was going, but I didn't need them hunting me down before I even landed. I would tell them about Seattle as soon as I got myself settled in. I packed my suitcase with as many items that would fit and then my carryon with my girly things. I figured what I didn't take, I would buy what I needed when I got there. I sent a few emails to some apartments I found online. I decided that I would deal with that when I landed. I laid down for a while but couldn't seem to fall asleep. I looked at the clock and it was almost four a.m. I tiptoed down the stairs and set my bags down by the door. I walked to the kitchen, turned on the light, and left the note on the counter by the coffee maker. I turned off the light, picked up my bags, opened the door, and headed down the drive towards the waiting cab.

I boarded the plane and suddenly became nervous. Since I couldn't remember if I had flown before, I considered this my first time and I was feeling anxious. I found my seat and sat down quickly. The flight wasn't so bad and the landing was smooth. I stepped outside and breathed in the Seattle air. I hailed a cab and had the cabbie drive me to the local Hilton. I put the key card in the door and turned the handle. I stepped into the room and admired the burgundy and beige décor while setting my suitcase on the bed. I pulled my phone from my purse and there was a text from Corinne.

*"Please be safe and call us the minute you get to your destination."*

I smiled because I expected some harsh words and a fight. But maybe they understood where I was coming from and decided to let me go.

*"I've landed and I'm safe. Please don't worry."*

I checked my email and found a response from one of the apartments I had inquired about. They had a one-bedroom apartment left that was ready for immediate occupancy. I dialed their phone number and told the girl on the phone I was on my way to look at it.

The cab pulled up to the three-story brown brick building, and I asked the driver if he could wait. He nodded his head and I headed inside to the rental office. As I stepped through the door, the manager held her finger up to me as she finished talking to someone on the phone. When she finished her conversation, she got out of her chair and introduced herself.

"I'm Tina, the manager of these apartments."

I extended my hand. "Hi, Claire Montgomery. I'm the one who called about the one-bedroom apartment for rent."

"Ah, yes, Miss Montgomery, follow me."

I followed the long-legged vixen up the stairs to the second floor. We walked down the long hallway until we reached 5B. Tina inserted the key in the lock, opened the door, and I stepped inside and looked around. The walls throughout were painted beige and the carpet looked brand new. The kitchen was an L-shape with a breakfast bar. The living room was spacious with two floor-to-ceiling windows. I walked down the short hallway to a half bath and across was the one bedroom with a private bath off to the side. Overall, the apartment was perfect and I didn't hesitate to let Tina know that I wanted it.

"Good choice, Claire. I know you'll love it here. Let's go down to my office and fill out the paperwork."

She told me I could move in that day, but I needed to buy some furniture first. I told her that I'd move in over the weekend. Just as we were leaving the apartment, and she was locking the door, a guy across the hall was leaving his apartment. He locked his door, said hi, and gave me a friendly smile. I would be lying if I said it was no big deal. This guy was gorgeous and he had a smile that would make any girl's heart flutter. Just what I needed, a hot guy living across the hall from me.

I stepped outside to the cab that was pulled up at the curb. I thanked him for waiting and asked him to take me to the closest furniture store. Once we arrived, I got out my money and paid him my cab fare. I told him it was okay to go and that I'd call another cab when I was ready to leave. I walked into Furniture for You and, instantly, a saleswoman approached me.

"Welcome to Furniture for You. What can I show you?"

I smiled. "I'm just looking right now, but if I need any help, I will let you know," I said as I squinted to see her name on her nametag. "Rose."

She nodded her head and walked away with a smile, but I could tell she was irritated. The first place I wanted to start was in the living room section. Instantly, I fell in love with a leather sofa in red and the matching chaise lounge. I found the perfect square coffee table and end table that complimented the style of the sofa. I searched the store for Rose because now I needed her help. As I was walking through the dining section, my heart stopped for a brief moment when I saw her talking to the guy that lived across the hall from me. *This was pure coincidence, right?* She walked away for a brief moment and he turned to examine a dining table I was pretty sure he had just bought. Okay, no big deal, I needed a dining room set too, so I walked over in that area to look at the sets. I caught him out of the corner of my eye, staring at me. I could feel it. I looked up as he walked towards me.

"Hi. Are we going to be neighbors?" He smiled shyly with his hands in his jean pockets.

"Hi. Yeah, I guess so."

I felt like an idiot and didn't know what else to say. I had to think quickly.

"Are you buying some furniture for your place?"

He smiled and my heart fluttered. Okay, this is not right; my heart shouldn't be fluttering. He took his hands out of his pocket.

"Yeah, I bought this table and chair set over here," he said as he motioned for me to follow him.

Sandi Lynn

I nodded my head as I ran my hand across the wood. "Nice set. Good taste." I smiled.

"I take it you're furniture shopping as well?"

"Yeah, I just moved here, and I don't have one piece of furniture."

I prayed he wouldn't ask me where I had moved from. He didn't. Rose walked up and handed him his credit card, receipt, and shook his hand. He smiled politely and thanked her for her help. I could tell she was smitten with him, the way she kept eyeing him up and down.

"Good bye, neighbor. If you need anything, you know where I live." He laughed lightly.

"Bye." I smiled as I gave him a small wave.

Rose lightly touched my arm. "Do you know him?"

"Nope. I rented the apartment across the hall from him, but I haven't moved in yet."

"He's so freaking hot and it seemed like he was into me. I have his number on the sales receipt. Maybe I'll call him and ask him out."

She was acting like a schoolgirl with a crush and she had to be at least ten years older than he was. I needed her to focus her attention on me and the furniture I wanted to purchase. I bit my bottom lip and was ready to break the poor woman's heart. "Umm, Rose? He's gay."

"Ugh, seriously?" she asked as she slouched her shoulders.

"Yeah. The manager of the building I'm moving into told me."

She looked like I had just killed her cat or something, but I thought the amount of money I was going to spend and the commission she'd make off it would cheer her up. I picked out everything I needed: the dining set, TV, living room set, bedroom set, and a few lamps. I was right; Rose was very pleased at her sale. As I was about to walk out of the store, I pulled my phone from my purse and saw I had a new voicemail message. I typed in my password and listened to it.

"Claire, it's Zoey. Mom told me what you did, and I can't believe you would just take off like that without any consideration for your family. Things never change, do they? Mom and Dad are really upset, and you need to call them. At least do that. Talk to you later."

I rolled my eyes as I walked out the doors of the furniture store. *What the hell did she mean 'things never change'?* I stopped as soon as my feet hit the sidewalk, for there was my new neighbor leaning up against his car with his arms folded.

"Umm, hi," I said shyly.

He gave me that shy smile and looked down. "Hi. I promise you I'm not a stalker."

Something inside told me he was harmless, but a girl can never be too careful.

"Okay, now that we've established you're not a stalker, may I ask why you're waiting out here?" I asked as I bit down on my bottom lip.

He shifted his body against the car. "When I left my apartment, I saw a cab at the curb and figured it was for you, so when I saw you here, and no cab, I thought I could maybe save you some money and give you a ride, since we're going to be neighbors and all."

Not only was he sexy to look at, but he was even sexier when he talked. There was a shyness about him that I found appealing. *Oh my God, what is wrong with me?* I'd only been in Seattle a few hours and some guy was already offering to give me a ride.

"It's okay. I'll just call a cab."

"I understand. New city, strange guy offering you a ride. I get it and, to be honest, I'm glad you said no because that means you're cautious and you should be."

Something about the way he said that was very sweet and comforting.

"I'll see you around the building," he said as he walked around to the driver's side and opened the door.

I didn't want him to leave. *Shit. What the fuck is the matter with me?*

"Hey, if you don't mind, I could use a ride to my hotel." The words escaped my lips and he smiled.

He walked over to the passenger's side and opened the door, motioning for me to get in. *Oh God, what was I doing?* His black Volvo was almost as sexy as he was. He got into the car, fastened his seatbelt, and held out his hand.

"I'm Sam. Sam Snow."

I extended my hand until it met his. "I'm Claire Montgomery, and it's nice to meet you, Sam Snow." I smiled.

Instantly, when our hands touched, a flash of light went off in my head. I pulled my hand away and held my head with both hands, looking down and breathing heavy. The pain was unbearable. My mind was flashing images of me shaking someone's hand in a car. I couldn't see their face, only their hand.

"Claire, are you okay?" Sam yelled.

After a few minutes, the pain subsided and my breathing started to become normal. Tears streamed down my face, and now, I was completely humiliated. I looked up at Sam, whose face and eyes showed pain and concern.

"What happened?" Sam asked.

I took in a sharp breath. "Sometimes, I get really bad headaches."

I sure as hell wasn't about to tell him anything else about me. I didn't even want to tell him that, but he did look concerned.

"Out of the clear blue like that?"

I looked out the window of the car. "Yes."

"Have you seen a doctor about those headaches?"

Okay, now he was getting a little too personal.

"I'm sorry, Sam, but I don't want to talk about it."

"I understand," he said as he started the car.

I felt bad, but I didn't know him, and I wasn't about to lay all my baggage on him. He seemed like a really nice guy and he didn't need me or my medical problems to complicate his life. I looked over at him and lightly touched his arm.

"Hey, I'm sorry, but it's hard to talk about, and I just want to take a hot shower."

"It's okay, Claire. There's no need to explain. I just want to make sure you're okay."

"I'll be fine, and thank you for your concern. I'm staying at the Hilton."

He started driving, one hand on the steering wheel, seat leaned slightly back; he was sexy and I couldn't stop looking at him. I had this overwhelming feeling being with him and it was something I couldn't explain.

"Do you know anybody here in Seattle?" he asked as he looked over at me.

"No, I don't," I replied.

He pulled up to the hotel and took a piece of paper and pen from his glove box. When he leaned over, his arm lightly brushed against my thigh.

"Here is my phone number. If you need anything or even just want to talk, please call me."

I took the paper from his hand. "Thank you, Sam, I appreciate it."

He smiled and made my heart flutter once again. I got out of the car, shut the door, and waved goodbye.

# *Chapter 10*

I turned on the shower as hot as it would go. The good thing about hotels is that they never run out of hot water. I stepped in and leaned my head back under the stream of water. I couldn't help but think of Sam and, every time I did, it made me smile. *Why was I thinking about him while I was in the shower?* He was the first person I met in Seattle and he was nice. Not to mention that he was hot as hell. I made a friend, and it was nice to say I knew someone here. I dried off my pruned skin and dug through my bag for my pills. My head was still aching so I took a pill, climbed into bed, and fell asleep.

I awoke the next morning as a beam of light radiated through the crack of the curtains. I looked over at the clock and saw that it was 9:15. My furniture was being delivered in two days and I still had a lot of things to buy. I looked at my phone and there were no new messages. I put on a pair of skinny jeans, a black tank top, and a pair of black flats. I brushed my teeth, threw some curls into my brown hair, and lightly put on some makeup. I grabbed my phone from the dresser and called a cab. I had the driver drop me off at the business district, which housed many retail businesses such as Crate and Barrel. I could smell the aroma of Starbucks coming from the street. There's nothing better than going shopping while sipping on a hot cup of java from Starbucks. I stepped inside and instantly, my eye veered to the corner, where I saw Sam sitting in an oversized burgundy chair, reading a book and drinking coffee.

He sat there in a pair of dark jeans and a navy blue fitted t-shirt. He was wearing black-rimmed square glasses that framed his chiseled face and his light brown hair was softly tousled. Good god, could he be any more perfect? Butterflies gathered in my stomach and fluttered every time I looked at him and it was driving me crazy. I rolled my eyes and shook my head. He looked up at me as I was awkwardly staring at him. He caught me off guard, so I quickly threw my hand up into a wave and ordered a venti white mocha skinny latte. As soon as they called my drink, I grabbed it from the counter and walked over to where Sam was sitting. He didn't take his eyes off me the entire time I waited for my coffee. He got up as I approached him and motioned for me to sit in the empty oversized chair next to him.

"Nice to see you, Miss Montgomery." He smiled, sending my heart into overdrive.

"Nice to see you too, Mr. Snow. What book are you reading?"

He looked so studious and smart in his glasses and my mind was going to places it shouldn't have. He held up a psychology book and smirked.

"Ah," I said with confusion.

Sam let out a light laugh. "I'm taking a psychology class over at the university."

I adjusted myself in the chair and crossed my legs. "Really?" I asked. "I was thinking about taking some classes there myself. That's why I rented the apartment so close to campus."

"Really?" he asked. "Then I'll show you around campus sometime if you'd like."

My small smile grew. "I'd like that."

He sat with his elbow on the arm of the chair and he took off his glasses. "What brings you to Starbucks today?"

"My caffeine addiction." I laughed softly. "Actually, I was on my way to Crate and Barrel."

"Ah, Crate and Barrel. Great store. Doing some more shopping?"

"Yeah. I don't have anything but furniture and I need to get the usual kitchen items, bath items, and—"

His beautiful blue-gray eyes stared directly at me. "I went through that not too long ago. It's a bitch of a shopping trip." He chuckled.

Here they come, the personal questions I never wanted to ask him because I didn't want to get too close.

"How long have you lived here?"

"Three months," he replied. "Hey, I have an idea," he said as he set his coffee down on the table. "If you don't mind, I'll take you to Crate and Barrel and then drive you back to your apartment so you can start putting things away. Kind of like getting a head start on organization."

Oh no, the butterflies that had settled down started to flutter again. I didn't want him to go with me, but then I did. I didn't know if it was because I was starting to feel a little scared here in a city all alone or if it was because I really wanted and needed a friend.

"That's okay. I don't want you to go to any trouble. I'm sure you have your own things to do."

"I have nothing to do today, and it's no trouble. Trust me; you'll be grateful to have me there." He looked down and smiled.

I couldn't help how the edges of my mouth curved up. "Is that so, Mr. Snow?"

His eyes danced as he lifted his head and looked at me. "Yes, Miss Montgomery. I'm sure you'll appreciate the help and not having to shove all those bags in a cab."

I got up from the oversized chair. "Okay, let's go then." I smiled.

His grin stretched across his face as he grabbed his coffee and followed me out the door.

\*\*\*\*

We spent over two hours in Crate and Barrel, and he was right: I was thankful he was with me, not only for the help, but for the company. I bought everything from small kitchen electrics to dinnerware, flatware, glasses, storage containers, bath items, a comforter for my new bed, pillows, sheets, blankets and decorative items for the apartment.

"Wow, aren't you glad I came with you?" he said as he gently bumped his fist into my arm.

"Yeah, yeah, yeah, you were right, and yes, I'm glad." I smiled.

He leaned over closer to me with his hand behind his ear.

"What? What was that, Claire? Did you say I was right?"

I laughed and jabbed my elbow into his arm to push him away. He put his hands in his pocket and smiled. We checked out and I spent an obscene amount of money. I knew it had to peak Sam's curiosity, but I was not about to share anything about my life with him; I just couldn't. Some of the stuff I purchased I was having delivered tomorrow and the rest we shoved into the trunk and back of Sam's car. He drove to the apartment and we started bringing the bags and boxes up one by one. I was out of breath and so was he when we brought the last of it up.

"Whew, that was my workout for the next three months," I said as I wiped the sweat from my forehead.

"No kidding. Some of that stuff was heavy." His navy blue shirt was drenched in sweat. "I'm going to run across the hall and change my shirt. I'll be right back, and then maybe we can grab some dinner?"

My stomach twisted itself in knots. I hadn't had anything to eat all day and I was starving. "Sounds like a plan." I smiled. This dinner thing didn't mean anything. I was hungry, and he was hungry, and that was what friends did; they ate together.

While I was waiting for Sam, I started to set up my kitchen. I put the coffeemaker on the counter and I continued to organize the cabinets. A while later, there was a knock at the door. I walked over, opened up the door, and gasped. Sam was standing there with his arms above, resting on the doorframe in his dark jeans and white button-down cotton shirt. Oh God, I hoped he didn't catch that gasp.

"Hi." He smiled at me.

"Hi."

"Are you ready to go?" he asked.

"Yes. Come in for a second while I get my things." I grabbed my purse and locked the door as Sam put his hand on the small of my back.

"I know this great pizza place down the street; that is, if you like pizza?"

"I like pizza." I smiled.

We approached Antonio's and sat in a comfy booth. The restaurant was a family-style parlor with tables decorated with black and white checked tablecloths. The floor was made up of black tile and black lights hung over each table.

"What should we order?" Sam asked as he looked at his menu.

"Hmm…pizza and salad?" I said as I looked up at him.

"Let me guess; you're a pineapple and ham type of girl."

I bit my bottom lip. "Yep; how did you know?"

"Girls usually are." He chuckled.

The tall, slender waitress came over to take our order and I could tell she was eyeing Sam.

"May I take your order?" she shyly asked with a big grin on her face.

"We'll have the large deep dish, half Hawaiian and half Italian sausage and green pepper."

She wrote down the order and continued to stare at Sam.

"Excuse me. Hello, over here." I waved at her.

The tall, slender waitress flinched and looked over at me.

"Add an antipasto salad to that order, please."

"Okay, anything else?" she asked.

Sam smiled at her and I could tell she was weak in the knees. "Two Cokes, please." She turned on her heels and walked away.

"Don't you ever get tired of women ogling you?" I asked.

He threw his head back and laughed. "What are you talking about?"

"Oh my God, she made it so obvious that she wanted you."

"No, she didn't." He smiled and his eyes lit up.

"By the way, I sort of told your saleslady at the furniture store that you were gay."

His eyes widened. "Why did you do that?"

"Well, she was going on and on about how you were looking at her. She said that she could tell you wanted her, and she was going to call and ask you out. She asked me if I knew you and I just kind of said you were gay."

Sam cocked his head and let out a chuckle. "You sound like you were jealous."

I gasped. "Jealous? No, she was a cougar."

"So." He smiled.

I looked at him and shook my head. *Was I jealous? Is that why I said he was gay?* No way could I be jealous; I barely knew him.

"So, where are you from, Claire Montgomery?" Sam asked as he leaned across the table.

Shit, I knew if I had to sit and have a conversation with him, he would start asking me personal questions. I had to think carefully and be cautious not to let anything real personal slip out.

"Newport Beach," I blurted out.

He raised his eyebrows and I put my hand up. "I know what you're thinking, but—"

"I'm from Santa Ana," he said as he cut me off.

I tilted my head to one side. "Really?"

"Yeah, I moved here three months ago to attend U of W."

I felt a sigh of relief when he told me he was from Santa Ana. Here were two young people that lived not too far from each other in California, living across the hall from each other, and going to attend the same university. In some way, I found that very comforting. He proceeded to tell me about his mom and Cal and how he worked as a mechanic to help support his family.

"Tell me about your family, Claire." He smiled.

My walls were up and that was how they were going to stay. "My dad, Harry, is a plastic surgeon. My mom, Corinne, does a lot of charity work, and my sister Zoey married a senator's son. That's about it."

"Tell me what it was like growing up in Newport Beach."

Okay, I had to stop this. He was getting too personal and I couldn't let him. Besides, how did I say that the only memory I had of my life was the past three years after my accident?

"It was fine," I lied. I needed to change the subject quickly. "Do you think you could drive me to the hotel so I can check out and grab my bags? I think I want to stay at the apartment tonight so I'm there first thing in the morning for the delivery truck."

His blue-gray eyes turned brighter. "Sure I can. That's a great idea."

The waitress brought over our bill, and when I went to grab it, Sam put his hand on top of mine. Instantly, I felt a surge run through my body. A feeling of warmth and safety pumped throughout my veins.

"My treat." He smiled.

I shook my head. "Sam, please let me pay for this. It's my thank you to you for everything you've done for me since I've been in Seattle, please. I gave him puppy eyes and he smiled.

"Fine, but the next one is on me."

He removed his hand from mine and I flipped over the bill. I rolled my eyes at how, Trish, our waitress, put her name and phone number on the bottom of the bill and wrote, "Call me." I held up the bill to Sam and he started laughing. Trish walked over when she saw the money on the table. She went to grab the bill and I put my hand on top of hers.

"Trish, I'm so sorry to tell you that he's gay." I smiled as I pointed to Sam.

She gasped, grabbed the bill, and scurried away. Sam stared at me with wide eyes and then busted out laughing. He was so beautiful when he laughed. I laughed with him as he put his hand on the small of my back and we walked out of Antonio's.

"I can't believe you did that, Claire." He laughed as he opened the car door for me.

"Yeah, well, she had it coming. She shouldn't be trying to pick up guys that are with a girl. What if I was your girlfriend or fiancée?" The words just fell out.

He got in the car and smiled at me. "Yeah, you're right."

I could tell he was thinking something, but I didn't want to know what it was. We drove to the hotel and took the elevator up to my room. The maid had been in, so it was spotless. I already had everything packed and Sam walked over to grab my bag.

"Is this it?" he asked.

"And this?" I said as I held up my carryon.

"Wow, Claire, you travel light."

"Everything I wanted to bring to Seattle is in these two bags."

"It seems to me like it was a last-minute decision and you're running from something."

I couldn't believe he said that, which wasn't far from the truth.

"Nope, I didn't want to drive seventeen hours by car, so I flew, and this was all I could bring."

He smiled and walked out the door with me following behind. I checked out, paid my bill, and Sam drove me to my apartment.

# *Chapter 11*

I opened the apartment door just as my phone started to ring. As I pulled it from my purse, I saw it was Zoey. I decided to answer it, even though I didn't want to talk in front of Sam. I put my bag down on the floor as he followed me into the apartment.

"Hello, Zoey."

"Claire, my baby shower is in a couple of weeks. Are you going to come home from whatever planet you're on to attend?" she said with irritation.

I cleared my throat. "Yes, Zoey. I'll be there. Give Mom and Dad big hugs from me, and I'll see you guys in a couple of weeks." *Click.*

I looked over at Sam, who was staring at me. "My sister is having a baby and her shower is in a couple of weeks. She wanted to know if I was going to make it home." *Why was I explaining this to him?*

"Baby shower? Sounds like fun." He smirked.

I saw him looking around the apartment. "Claire, where are you going to sleep?"

"I have blankets I'll set on the floor. I'll be fine."

He looked at me with a sexy look, but I didn't think he realized it. "Let me help you put some of this stuff away," he said as he saw me rummaging through bags. "First, we need some music." He pulled out his iPhone from his pocket and, suddenly, Coldplay started playing. Bright lights flashed in my mind, blinding me as I grabbed the sides of my head and fell to the ground on my knees. Sam came rushing over as he dropped down beside me and pulled me into his arms. I kept my eyes tightly closed as images of a car and that same song played over the radio. I was in the passenger's seat, but I couldn't see who was driving. The music played as we both sang to it. Sam rocked me back and forth and I wanted to die right there in his arms.

The pain stopped, the lights went away, and my mind went dark. Tears rolled down my face as I held onto Sam's arms.

"Claire," he whispered. He leaned back so he was fully lying on the ground, but he didn't let me go. I moved back with him and we both fell asleep as he held me.

My eyes jerked open, and I looked down and found that Sam had his arm draped around my waist. I looked over at him and his eyes opened.

"Good morning." He smiled.

I jumped up. "Sam, what the hell! Why did you stay here all night?"

"I needed to make sure you were okay. I wasn't going to leave you like that."

The headaches seemed to be coming more frequently since I moved to Seattle. "I appreciate that Sam, but it's not your responsibility to take care of me," I snapped at him.

He got up and looked at me with hurt in his eyes. "I'm sorry, Claire, but I'm your friend, and friends look out for each other. I would hope that if something happened to me, you would look out for me."

I dropped my shoulders and sighed. He was right and I was being nothing but a cold-hearted bitch. I walked over to where he was standing and put my hand on his heart.

"You have a kind and warm heart, Sam Snow. Thank you."

He smiled and my heart melted, especially when he was standing there with messed up morning hair, looking as hot as ever.

"Do you have any coffee?" I asked as I bit down on my bottom lip.

"I sure do. I'll go grab some and bring it over."

"Thank you," I said as I lifted my hand from his rock hard chest.

He walked over to his place, and I got in the shower. I stood and let the hot water run down my body as I thought about my episode from last night. I found it odd that as soon as Sam turned on Coldplay, the headache started. I must have been listening to that song, because what I saw was a glimpse of a memory, I know it was. But who was driving the car and singing with me? So many questions and so few answers; actually, no answers. I opened my eyes when I heard a door shut.

"Sam," I called.

"Yeah, it's just me. I brought the coffee. I'll start a pot."

I reached over for the shampoo, but I forgot to put anything in the shower. No soap, shampoo, razor, nothing. SHIT. Reluctantly, I called for Sam.

"Sam."

"Yeah," he yelled.

"Can you please go in my small bag and grab my shampoo, conditioner, body soap, and razor?"

I heard him laugh. "Sure."

He knocked on the bathroom door, which was half open, and I was humiliated.

"Umm, here?"

"Just set it down on the ledge there," I said.

I could feel him smiling. He walked out and, after I was done with my shower, I wrapped myself in a towel and looked around the bathroom. For fuck's sake, I didn't bring any clothes in with me.

"Sam, could you please turn around? I need to get some clothes."

He laughed. "Okay, I'm not looking."

I stepped out of the bathroom and looked down the hall to make sure Sam wasn't looking. I ran to my bedroom and shut the door. I got dressed and, as I brushed my wet hair, the buzzer to my apartment rang.

"I got it, Claire." Sam yelled.

When I stepped out of the bedroom, I saw two burly guys bringing in the boxes of things I'd bought. The coffee was done brewing and I took two cups from the cupboard and filled them to the top. I looked at Sam as I handed him a cup.

"I hope you like it black because I didn't go to the grocery store and I don't have any cream or sugar."

He smiled lightly. "Black is fine." He held his coffee cup up, brought it to mine, and lightly clanked them together.

"Here's to your new move to Seattle. I hope you'll like it here."

I smiled. *I'll like it here as long as he lives across the hall,* I thought to myself.

"Claire, I know you don't want to talk about it, but I really think you should see a doctor about those headaches."

*Here we go again. He won't give up, will he?*

"Sam, I've seen doctors, many doctors, and they don't know what's wrong. As long as I have my pills, I'll be fine.

"No, you won't be fine. I've never seen anyone in pain like that before."

"It's not that bad," I lied.

"The hell it isn't," he said with irritation. "Last night was the second time I saw you like that and, to be honest, it scared the fuck out of me."

"I'm sorry, Sam, but if we're going to continue to be friends, then you'll have to get used to it and stop asking me questions because I'm not going to give you any answers," I snapped.

There, I said it. I made it perfectly clear that I was not opening up my life to him. His face looked pained and it hurt my heart to see him standing there like that. He put his coffee cup down on the counter.

"I've got to go home and shower. I have class in a couple of hours. I'll see you around, Claire."

I didn't say a word as he walked out of my apartment, shutting the door behind him. Tears started to sting my eyes. I hurt him on a deeper level. I could tell, but I couldn't let him get close to me. He deserved more and better than me. I tried to forget about our conversation and spent the day putting everything away and getting organized for the delivery of my furniture tomorrow. Since I needed to fill my refrigerator, I stepped out of the apartment and walked down the street to a small grocery shop that sat on the corner. I grabbed a basket and picked up a few items. I could only buy enough that I could carry back.

When I was finished and, as I walked out of the store, I noticed a guitar shop across the street. I waited for traffic to clear, walked across to the store, and went inside.

"You can set those bags down here on the counter if you want to look around," a man who was covered in tattoos said.

"Thank you." I smiled.

He stood about six feet tall, slender build, long black hair, and dark brown, mysterious eyes. Both arms were covered in tattoos; mostly religious tattoos of crosses and verses from the Bible. I walked over to the guitars that lined the walls. I loved the way guitars sounded when you strummed the strings.

"See anything you like?" the man said behind me.

My eye caught a Gibson Montana in vintage sunburst. After the accident, I would hide in my room and practice the guitar for hours every day along with the piano. The guitar and piano became my life and the music helped with my depression.

"Can I try that one?"

"You sure can. Been playing long?"

"About three years," I answered.

He lifted the guitar off the hook from the wall and handed it to me. I ran my hand down the neck and around the base, getting a feel for it before I started to pluck the strings. This guitar felt right. I sat down and sat the guitar in my lap, holding it and positioning my fingers on the fret. I strummed each string as I switched notes. I smiled as I started to strum a tune I wrote back in Newport Beach. I saw the clerk smiling; his eyes closed as he took in every note I played.

"Music washes away from the soul the dust of everyday life."

I stopped playing and looked at him with a smile. "Berthold Auerbach's quote."

"Very good, little lady." He winked at me.

"And he's right. It does." I stood up and handed him the guitar. "I'll take it with that case over there and some guitar picks."

"Great choice in guitars, little lady, and let me say that you really have a talent."

"Thank you." I smiled as I paid him.

I grabbed the case with the guitar in it and fumbled to hold the two bags of groceries. I smiled and walked out. Thank God my apartment was only around the block because I wasn't going to be able to hold onto these groceries much longer. Just as I was approaching the building, a nice little old lady held the door open for me.

"Good day, dear. I see you have your hands full. Do you need some help?"

"No, thank you. I can manage." I smiled.

"You're the girl who moved in across the hall from Sam, aren't you?"

I smiled as I looked at her. "Yes, I'm Claire Montgomery."

"I'm Ida Whitfield, honey, nice to meet you. Sam told me about you."

"Is that so?" I said as I cocked my head to the side.

Ida smiled. "No worries, honey. It was nothing but all good. I live right here in 1A. Come down sometime for coffee and biscuits and we can have a chat, get to know each other better."

"Thank you, Ida, I will, but now I have to get this stuff upstairs."

I walked up the stairs. Boy did I need to work out, especially my legs. I set one bag down as I reached in my pocket for my keys. I opened the door, grabbed my bag of groceries, and kicked the door shut behind me. I put everything away and looked at the guitar case propped up against the wall. I heard a door shut from across the hall and sensed Sam had just gotten home. I was missing him and I hated myself for letting me feel this way. I couldn't stop thinking about last night and the way he held me while I cried and how he stayed with me all night to make sure I was okay. *Was he falling for me?* I knew damn well I was falling for him, and it scared the shit out of me. I didn't know if I'd ever fallen for a guy before. At least if I did, I didn't remember, and I had a hard time believing my family and friends when I asked. I picked up my phone and dialed Rachel.

"Claire, hi, how are you? Where are you? Are you okay?"

Rachel had a habit of just rambling on and not letting anyone get a word in.

"I'm fine Rachel. I'm in Seattle getting settled into my new apartment, and I wanted to call and say hi."

"Aw, Claire, you sound sad and lonely," she whined.

"I'm fine, Rachel, and I mean that. You and Ally are going to have to come here and visit me."

"We'd love to. Have you met anyone there yet?"

I hesitated to tell her about Sam. "I just met the guy across the hall and Ida who lives downstairs."

I heard excitement in her voice. "So, tell me about this guy across the hall. Is he hot? Is he sexy? What's his name?"

I laughed. "Rachel, he is very nice looking, and that's all you need to know right now."

"Claire Montgomery, spill now!" she demanded.

"Listen, there's nothing to spill. He helped me out with some boxes and that's it. He's a nice guy. Anyway, I need to ask you something."

"Shoot," she said.

"I know I've asked you this before, but are you sure I wasn't seeing someone before the accident?"

There was a hint of hesitation in her voice. "No, Claire. You weren't seeing anyone. You always said the guys you were attracted to were too immature and spoiled."

I sighed.

"Why are you asking anyway?" she asked.

"Since I moved here, my headaches and memory flashes have gotten worse, and I had one last night with me in a car sitting next to someone and we were singing Coldplay together. It was a man's voice, Rachel."

"I don't know, Claire, maybe it was your dad or Dylan. I don't know, sweetie, but I have to go. I have to leave for work. I'll call you soon. Love you."

And just like that, she was gone. I held up the phone and stared at it. That was weird and I could sense a nervousness in her voice.

# *Chapter 12*

I walked over to the guitar case, flipped the latches, and lifted the cover, exposing my new guitar. I smiled as I took it out and then sat down, leaning up against the wall. I strummed a few chords, noticing how tuned the guitar already was, compliments of the tattoo guy at the store. I started strumming the song "Winter" which was one of my favorite songs to play. I closed my eyes and played the entire tune, thinking about what the guy from the guitar store said.

*"Music washes away from the soul the dust of everyday life."*

I always got lost when I played the guitar or the piano. I liked being transported to a world of my own where nothing could touch me or hurt me. I felt safe in my music world and that was where I went when I needed to escape and be alone. Suddenly, I was startled by a knock at the door.

"Clair, it's Ida from downstairs."

I got up from the floor and opened the door.

"Hello, dear. Was that you playing that beautiful song?"

"Yes, I'm so sorry if I disturbed you."

"No, dear, I just had to come up and tell you how beautiful it was."

I smiled and invited her in. She looked over my shoulder and saw an empty apartment.

"How about you come down to my place and bring that guitar with you? I would love for you to have some dinner with me. It can get kind of lonely by myself sometimes."

As much as I didn't want to bother her, I looked around my empty apartment. I grabbed my guitar, slipped on my shoes, and followed her downstairs. Her apartment was the same layout as mine. Her furniture was floral patterned that looked like it was from the seventies. She had little crocheted doilies on each table, and pictures of her children and grandchildren were scattered all over the place. It was your typical little old lady home.

"What's that smell?" I asked.

"My homemade chicken soup. There isn't anything like it. Come sit down, dear, and let me make you some tea."

Ida stood about five feet tall. She kept her white hair pulled back neatly in a bun and her eyes were blue in color. Her skin was wrinkly and she didn't wear any makeup. I sat at the table as she made tea for the both of us.

"Tell me about yourself, dear," she said as she placed my teacup in front of me.

"There isn't much to tell. I'm from Newport Beach, I have one sister, and I moved here to attend U of W."

She sat down and steadily put her cup on the table. "So tell me what you think of Sam."

I looked at her. "He's been very nice and helpful to me."

"Nice boy he is. I'd say he'd make a great husband to someone someday. He's always down here fixing something for me or running an errand. That boy has the genes of a saint."

I wanted to roll my eyes because I knew what she was trying to do. What she didn't know was that I already knew what she was telling me was true, and I was trying hard to forget it.

"Do you have a boyfriend?" she asked.

I smiled gently at her. "No, I don't have a boyfriend. To be honest with you, Ida, I don't want one either."

"Psh," she said as she waved her hand. "Everyone needs somebody. It's the way life is. You can't live by yourself your whole life. It's a lonely road, my dear."

I gave her a half smile as I took a sip of my tea. A few moments later, there was a knock at the door. Ida got up and opened it. I turned around and there was Sam standing in the doorway with a small bag in his arms.

"Is that chicken soup I smell, Ida?" He smiled as he gave her a kiss on the cheek.

"It sure is, Sam. Come on in. Look who's here."

He glanced at me. I could tell he was uncomfortable and I hated myself for making him feel that way. "Hi, Claire," he said as he walked over and set the bag on the counter.

"Hi, Sam." I smiled.

"What is this, Sam?" Ida asked.

"I was at the store and just picked you up a few things."

My heart melted and tears sprang to my eyes. This man was so perfect and so sweet to others and I treated him like shit. I looked down as Ida walked over to him. She cupped his face in her hands.

"You are the son I never had, and I love you, Sam Snow. Now sit down and I'll get you some tea."

He gave her a warm smile. "Ida, I have to go. I have…"

"Nonsense," she cut him off. "You're going to stay and have soup with me and Claire and I don't want to hear another word about it," she said in an authoritative tone.

"Yes, ma'am," he said as he sat down next to me.

"Sorry," I mouthed.

He gave me half of a smile. A half of a smile that filled my heart with warmth and made my stomach flutter.

"Sam, did you know this pretty little lady can play the guitar?"

He looked at me with those smoldering blue-gray eyes and said, "No, I didn't know that."

"Well, she can. Go ahead, dear, play something for us."

"Yeah, play something for us, Claire." He smiled.

I rolled my eyes at him, got up, and grabbed my guitar.

"Nice guitar. Wow, Claire, she's a beauty."

"Thanks, I just got it today at the music store down the street."

"So you met Al?"

"If you're referring to the man with a million tattoos, then yes."

"He's a good man, and wise too," Sam said.

"Yeah, he was great and really helpful."

I strummed my guitar and thought about what to play. I strummed a few chords and headed into a song. Sam stared into my eyes and started singing the lyrics.

"All I ever knew, only you."

I started to sing with him and, before I knew it, we were singing together. His voice was angelic and each note he sang was perfect. I ended the song with a strum and he smiled.

"Joshua Radin is one of my favorites."

I gasped because, at that moment, that very moment, everything I believed about Sam became real. Ida got up from her seat and wiped her eyes.

"You two made me cry," she said as she placed bowls of soup in front of us.

"Sorry, Ida. We didn't mean to." Sam smiled.

We sat around the table and talked mostly about Ida and her family. She told us how she found and married her soul mate and had three children, twelve grandchildren, and five great-grandchildren. Before I knew it, three hours had passed.

"Well, Ida, I think it's time for us to leave. It's getting pretty late," Sam said as he got up.

I hugged Ida goodbye and thanked her for the delicious soup. Sam did the same and put his hand on the small of my back as we walked out the door. We both walked up the stairs and, as we approached our apartments, Sam said good night and inserted his key. I needed to apologize for how I acted earlier and now was as good as time as any.

"Sam."

He turned around and looked at me before opening his door. "Yeah, Claire."

I took in a sharp breath. "I want to apologize for earlier. I'm sorry for the things I said. You didn't do anything to deserve that," I said as I looked down.

He walked toward me and lifted my chin with his hand. "It's okay. I crossed the line, and for that, I'm sorry."

I shook my head because what he said wasn't true. "No, Sam, you didn't. You're concerned like any friend would be, and I turned on you."

His beautiful eyes stared into mine as he leaned his face closer and softly brushed my lips with his. My heart started beating rapidly as I prayed to God my head wouldn't start hurting. He looked at me to be sure it was okay, and I smiled, taking his lips to mine and parting them as I felt his tongue enter. My body started to get weak, and I wanted more of him, even though I knew it wasn't a good idea. He pulled away from my lips and hugged me tight.

"I've wanted to do that since the first day I saw you."

I became weak as he said that, and in that moment, I knew I was done for.

"Could you do something for me?" he asked.

"Anything. What is it?"

"Stay at my place tonight, totally as friends, no sex, nothing. I just don't like the thought of you sleeping there on the hard floor. You can have my bed and I'll take the couch."

I smiled because the thought was so appealing, and I didn't really want to be alone with nothing in the apartment. "I don't think that's a good idea."

His hands gripped my hips. "You're right, Claire. It's not a good idea; it's a great idea, and it's not up for discussion. I won't let you sleep on the floor. Now, tell me that you like the idea."

I sighed as I stared into his pleading eyes. "I like that idea very much, Sam. Thank you for the offer." He was grinning from ear to ear as he softly kissed me.

"Okay, go get what you need and come over. You don't have to knock; you can just walk in."

I gave him a hug before stepping into my apartment. "I'll be there soon."

I ran to the bathroom and changed into a pair of black cotton pajama bottoms from Victoria's Secret and a matching t-shirt. I put my hair up in a high ponytail, grabbed my phone charger, and walked over to Sam's apartment. I walked in and saw him standing in the kitchen, washing some dishes.

"Ah, trying to clean up before the girl comes over?" I laughed.

"I guess you could say that."

Sam's apartment was nice. His walls were the same color beige as mine. His living room was done in black leather furniture with glass tables and a plasma TV attached to the wall.

"I like your place, Mr. Snow."

"Thank you, Miss Montgomery. I must say you are looking very cute in your pajamas." He winked.

I laughed and lightly tapped him on the arm.

"Would you like to watch a movie?" he asked shyly.

"Sure. What movie?"

"We can rent whatever you want from the TV."

He walked over, grabbed the remote, and turned on the TV. He scrolled through the new movies and we agreed on a romantic comedy.

"No movie is complete without popcorn," he said.

I followed him into the kitchen and he microwaved some popcorn. I noticed a picture of him and an older woman on the refrigerator.

"Is that your mom?"

"Yeah, that was taken right before I left."

"She's pretty." I smiled.

Sam took the popcorn out of the microwave and opened the bag.

"Ouch," he said as he dropped the bag on the counter.

"Are you okay?"

"Just a little steam burn," he pouted.

I grabbed his hand and held it under the cold water. He stared at me with a grin. I took his hand and wrapped it in a towel to dry it. I removed the towel, brought his hand to my lips, and gently kissed the spot where he burned himself.

"There, all better."

"You'd make a great nurse, Claire." He smiled as he brought his hand to my cheek.

The touch of his bare skin set my body on fire. I desired this man in every way possible and it scared me. The feeling of being half a person was awful and Sam deserved so much more. I finished putting the popcorn in the bowl and we sat on the couch, watching the movie. He put his arm on the back of the couch and I nestled into him. I hated to admit that when I was with him, I felt whole and complete. I was headed for trouble and heartache, and I knew it. Nothing can last forever. Your life can change in an instant, and before you know it, everything you've known and loved is gone.

# *Chapter 13*

The garden was beautiful, and I felt so much peace. "If your love was true, you will find each other again." I kept hearing someone whisper those words over and over. I was pulled back into darkness until the bright lights started flashing in my head. Images of the beach kept playing over and over in my mind. I heard the same crash again and again. I started shaking and heard a voice whisper, "Claire, wake up; it's only a dream. Wake up, baby. Please."

I awoke curled in a fetal position on the floor, with my hands covering my ears and tears streaming down my face. Sam was kneeling in front of me with his arms wrapped around me. I grabbed a hold of his arm and buried my head into his chest.

"I can't take this anymore," I cried. "This has to stop. I'm going crazy, Sam."

"Ssh … it was a bad dream, Claire. I'm here, and I'm not going to let anything happen to you."

I pushed him away and he fell back. "It wasn't a dream, Sam; it's my reality, my living hell." I stood up and turned my back so I wouldn't have to look at him. I didn't want to see the disappointment and the hurt on his face.

"Let it be my hell too, Claire. Share your life with me. Tell me what happened to you. For fuck's sake, Claire. Let me help you."

I froze and shook my head. "I can't let you help me. I'm so fucked up and broken, there's nothing anyone can do to save me, and I won't drag you into my hell," I cried and flew out of his apartment and into mine. I curled up on my blanket and cried the rest of the night. Sam didn't come after me.

The next morning, the delivery truck arrived and delivered my furniture. They were kind enough to set the furniture exactly where I told them to. My heart ached so badly and my eyes were red and swollen from crying all night. I felt like I'd been hit by a truck. Once again, I fucked things up with Sam. *Could life be any worse by letting him in my life?* I was already living in my own personal hell, but when I was with him, it felt like heaven. I wanted to feel like that every day. I'd longed for that feeling since the accident. Sam wanted to give me that and, each time, I pushed him away.

I looked around my newly furnished apartment and tried to smile. Everything was in its place and this was now a home, my home. There was one more thing I needed to do. It didn't matter anymore. I couldn't feel any worse and I needed to try and feel better.

I ran across the hall and pounded on Sam's door. He answered wearing only a pair of navy blue pajama bottoms that hung slightly off his hips. I started to quiver when I saw him. His muscular chest was rock hard and his six-pack was beautifully defined. He looked at me differently than he ever had. His eyes looked cold and dark, not his usual warm and bright blue-gray. He didn't say a word and he didn't invite me in. I pushed through the door.

"Claire, what are you doing?"

I put my hand up and turned around. I noticed he had about a two-inch scar from his belly button, down around his right side. It looked like a surgical scar of some sort. I closed my eyes and took in a deep breath.

"I was in a very bad car accident that pretty much left me dead. I actually died for three minutes and, when I was brought back, I had no memory of my life. The only people I barely remembered were my Mom, Dad, and Zoey. Seventeen years of living gone in a flash." Tears started to fill my eyes.

Sam stood there for a moment with a look of shock on his face. He started to walk over to me and I stopped him. "Don't; please let me finish. Since the accident, I get these flashes of bright lights in my head and blurred images. I think they might be memories, but I'm not sure. That's when the headaches start." Sam came over to me, wrapped his arms around me, and kissed my head.

"My God, Claire. I'm so sorry."

I started to cry into his shoulder. "Don't you see? I only have three years of my life I can share with you. I can't share my childhood with you because I can't remember it. I'm a stranger in my own body."

He picked me up and carried me to his bedroom, where he laid me down on his bed and continued to hold me. As I faced him, I ran my finger up and down his scar.

"What happened to you?" I sniffled.

Sam kissed my cheek. "I'll tell you another time," he said as he stroked my hair.

I looked up at his face that showed great concern for me. "I moved here because I couldn't live in that house anymore. For the past three years, I've felt like a stranger in the house I grew up in. I needed to start my own life. I needed to try and find me, if that makes sense."

Sam pushed the stray hairs away from my face. "It makes perfect sense, and I'm glad you chose Seattle."

I had just bared my soul to him and now we were bonded in the way I swore I never would be with anyone. I desired him and longed to feel him inside me. The attraction was there the minute I saw him. I lifted my head and traced his lips with my finger. As he smiled, my heart started to race. I sat up and lifted my shirt over my head, tossing it on the floor. Sam took in a sharp breath.

"You're so beautiful, Claire."

I leaned over and kissed his lips. I didn't have to ask him to make love to me. He already knew that I wanted him to. He took his hands and slowly undid my bra, throwing it over the side of the bed. His hands moved freely over my breasts, cupping each one, giving special attention to my nipples. Sam broke our kiss and looked at me.

"Are you sure?" he asked.

"It's the first thing I've ever been so sure of in my life," I whispered.

He gently pushed me back to a lying position and he hovered over me. My hands moved up and down his back as he softly kissed my neck and his tongue made its way to my throat. I tilted my head back so he could have better access. I could feel his erection against me as he gently tugged at each nipple, then softly licked them to soothe the sting. His hand moved down my torso and took down my pants. As I lifted myself to help him, he gently pushed his fingers through the sides of my panties. A soft moan came from the back of his throat as he felt the wetness that was caused by him. His lips found mine as he gently inserted his finger inside me and slowly rubbed my clit in circles with his thumb. I moaned and pushed my hips up as he gently pushed another finger inside. He was gentle and made me feel safe. His strokes were undeniably arousing me as my body started to tighten and my breathing became rapid. It felt like an earthquake was going to erupt inside me as my moans became louder.

My hands reached the waistband of his pajama bottoms and took them down while grabbing his perfectly shaped ass. His lips left mine and moved over to each breast, down my stomach to my navel, and then to my aching spot that wanted him so badly. As his tongue made its way to my clit, both he and I could feel me swell as I couldn't hold back anymore.

"Come for me, Claire. Come for me," he whispered.

Just the words were enough to send me into oblivion. I screamed as the orgasm rippled through my body and I began shaking. He made his way back up to me.

"I have condoms." He smiled.

"I'm on the pill, Sam, but I think we should still use a condom anyway."

He smiled at me and reached for his wallet. He tore open the condom and sat up, pulling it over his hard cock. He looked at me before he took my mouth to his, kissing me hard and passionately. I wrapped my legs around him as he grabbed his cock and gently pushed it inside me. We both moaned at the same time. I grabbed his hair and moved my hands through it as he thrust in and out of me, slowly. I dug my nails into his back, which made him thrust harder and faster and I screamed his name as I could feel myself building up for another orgasm.

"Come with me, baby. I want to hear you," he panted.

Finally, I reached my peak as he pushed himself deep inside me, saying my name while staring into my eyes. I held his face as I whispered his name and my orgasm exploded. He fell on top of me and we lay there, feeling each other's hearts pounding against our bare skin. That was the most beautiful experience I had ever felt. Instantly, nothing else mattered in my life except Sam.

After he got up, removed the condom, and discreetly disposed of it in the bathroom, he smiled at me as he walked towards the bed, holding out his hand and signaling for me to join him in the shower, where we made love again.

I had to go back to my apartment to get dressed and I told him to come over as soon as he was ready. I stood in the bathroom, looking in the mirror, wondering if I had ever made love to anyone before. I heard the door open and, suddenly, there were two arms wrapped around me.

"Hi, baby." He smiled.

I looked at him through the mirror. "Can I ask you something?"

"Sure. Shoot!"

I didn't know how to ask, so I was just going to say it. "Do you think I was a virgin?"

Sam looked at me in the mirror and then turned me around so I was facing him. "Why do you ask?"

"Because I want to know. You don't know how frustrating it is to have these experiences and not know or remember if you've ever felt it before."

He looked down. "No, I don't think you were, and I do know, well, sort of know what you're going through."

I cocked my head to the side. "What do you mean?"

He took my hand and led me to my bedroom. "Sit down," he said.

I sat on the bed, my heart racing and stomach tied in knots, not knowing what he was going to say.

"This scar you saw," he said as he lifted his shirt. "It's from a car accident I was in about three years ago." I gasped and put my hand over my mouth.

"I had to have a kidney transplant, and when I woke up after I was in a coma for a few days, I had no memory of the year prior to the accident."

Tears swelled in my eyes. Sam kneeled down in front of me and grabbed my hands. "Don't cry, babe. Please. That was the past, and both of us are moving forward together; that's if you want to do this together. Please, no more tears."

I brought my hand to his cheek and stared into his beautiful eyes. "This is so strange, Sam. I feel like fate brought me here to you. Two people with the same problems. I'm sort of freaked out right now." I laughed.

He chuckled and he pulled me into an embrace. "Yeah, it's strange, but let's take advantage of it. You're here, I'm here, and we're definitely attracted to each other. Fate works in mysterious ways, Claire."

My phone started to ring and, when I looked at it, I saw it was Corinne.

"Hi, Mom." I answered.

"Hi, Claire. I was just making sure you'll be here on time for your sister's baby shower."

"Yeah, I'll be there, no worries."

"Claire, you sound different."

"I am, Mom. This move was good for me. I finally feel like I'm where I'm supposed to be."

"A man wouldn't have anything to do with that, would he?" I wasn't ready to divulge any information about Sam.

"Let's just say I've met someone, and I think he's really special." I winked as I looked at Sam.

"That's great, Claire. We would like to meet him sometime. Maybe Daddy and I could come visit you."

That was the last thing I wanted right now. "We can talk about it when I come home for the shower. Tell Dad I love him, and I love you, Mom."

"We love you too, sweetheart. See you soon."

I hung up with her and looked at Sam. He took my hand and led me to the living room.

"Let's go out to eat. I'm starving," he said.

"Sounds like a plan. I'm hungry too." I smiled as I grabbed my purse, looped my arm in his, and walked out the door.

While we were in the restaurant, Sam smiled at me from across the table. "I have an idea. Let's go back to California together. You can attend your sister's baby shower, and I can visit my mom."

My eyes started dancing with delight. "That's a great idea. I can book our flights."

He smirked in a sexy way that sent chills throughout my body. "No planes; we're going to drive. Consider it a little road trip."

"You do realize it's a seventeen-hour drive, right?"

"Yep, and I want to spend all seventeen hours of it sitting next to you."

I leaned over and kissed him. "I love that idea."

# *Chapter 14*

I prepared dinner for me and Sam and I waited for him to get back from class. He opened the door to my apartment, put his book bag down, and wrapped his arms around me, kissing me from behind. "How was your day, babe?" he asked.

"Lonely without you." I pouted.

He laughed and leaned against the counter. "I spoke with Dr. Benjamin today."

"Who's that?" I asked.

"He's a neurosurgeon who teaches a class at the university. He wants to see you. He said he might be able to help you."

"Sam, I've been to see so many doctors and no one has any answers."

He grabbed my waist, pulling me closer to him. "Look, it doesn't hurt to talk to him. I'll be with you, so you don't have to be nervous."

A warmness crept inside me. It meant the world to me that Sam wanted to help me and I didn't want to set him up for disappointment. But, I couldn't refuse his help because it meant so much to him. I tapped his nose with my finger. "Fine, I'll see him."

"Good, because he's coming over for dinner. He'll be here in an hour."

"Sam Snow!" I yelled.

He ducked from my wrath and went to the bathroom. I was making spaghetti, so there was plenty of food. A few moments later, Sam emerged from the bathroom with his hands up.

"Are we cool?" He smiled.

"Yeah, but you can make the salad."

He nuzzled against me and whispered in my ear, "I'm good at making a lot of things."

I smiled. "Salad, now."

He laughed and walked to the refrigerator, grabbing the items for the salad.

****

Dr. Benjamin stood around six feet, two inches, with a medium build and salt and pepper hair. He reminded me of Dr. Oz. We sat at the dinner table and talked first about his career and family. He propped his elbows on the table and crossed his hands.

"Claire, I want you to have an MRI. We need to see how your brain has healed. I believe what you're experiencing with these flashes of light and images are true memories that are trying to force their way back, but something is stopping them."

I looked at him and cocked my head in confusion.

"It could be anything from a tumor, scar tissue, or maybe your subconscious doesn't want to remember."

"That's ridiculous, doctor. Of course I want to remember my life."

"You told me that no one in your family would give you straight answers about your life prior to the accident and that you felt they were hiding something."

"I don't know, Dr. Benjamin; maybe I was just being paranoid."

He got up from the table. "Sam tells me you two are heading back home for a few days. I really would like you to get that MRI done before you leave. Can you come in tomorrow at one p.m.?"

I looked over at Sam as he nodded his head. "Yes, she'll be there tomorrow."

"Yes, I'll be there tomorrow." I smiled.

"Perfect. Thank you for dinner. It was delicious, and it was nice meeting you. I shall see you tomorrow, Claire."

Sam walked over and kissed me on my forehead. "Thank you. I know he can help you."

"I hope so," I said as I hugged him. "We need to make love." I smiled.

"Then let's go." He grinned as he took my hand and led me to the bedroom.

We made passionate love, and every time felt like the first. He was amazing and so passionate; it was like our bodies were made to fit one another perfectly. This was my life now, and my memories; nothing else mattered. Maybe Dr. Benjamin was right and I didn't want to remember. *What could've happened to me?* I closed my eyes and tightened my grip on Sam's arm, which was holding me tight. It wasn't too long before I drifted to sleep.

I was in the courtyard with Ally and Rachel, eating the lunch they had brought me. I was scrolling through pictures on Rachel's phone and saw the picture of me and someone, but the image of the person who had his arm around me was blurry.

*"Oh, that's my cousin. You two were good friends,"* she said.

I lifted up her phone closer to my eyes, trying to make the picture clear. My head started pounding and suddenly the picture came into focus. I gasped when I saw it and I dropped the phone. The boy sitting next to me in the picture was Sam.

"Babe, wake up; you're having a bad dream," I heard Sam say.

I sat up straight with tears in my eyes and my hair wet from sweat. Sam tried to put his arm around me, but I pulled back and got out of bed. My heart was racing and it felt like it was trying to jump out of my chest.

"Claire, what is it?"

I put my hand over my mouth as I stared at him. Sam jumped out of bed and came over to me.

"Claire, talk to me, NOW! Dammit, you're scaring me."

I held up my finger and searched for my phone. I found it on the dresser and dialed Rachel's number.

"Claire, it's three o'clock in the morning. Who the hell are you calling?"

"Hello. Claire, it's the middle of the night. What's wrong?" a sleepy voice answered.

"Rachel, I need your help. You have to help me. Remember when you and Ally came to the hospital and we were in the courtyard and you were showing me pictures on your phone?"

"Yeah," she spoke hesitantly.

"Remember when I came across the one with me and your cousin?"

"Yeah. Claire, what's this about?"

"He wasn't your cousin, was he? Was he, Rachel? And don't you dare lie to me." I started trembling.

"Claire, I can't talk about this now."

"Do you still have that picture?"

"That was three years ago. I don't have that phone anymore."

"Rachel, you said that you and Ally have been my best friends since we were five years old. You would never lie to me would you?"

"Claire, I'll call you in a few hours. Please go to sleep," she said before she hung up.

She was gone and I knew in that instant she was lying to me. I set my phone down.

"What the fuck is going on, Claire?" Sam exclaimed.

"Rachel had a picture on her phone of me and some guy. She told me it was her cousin and that we were good friends, but the guy in the picture was you, Sam," I said as I trembled.

He brushed his hands through his hair. "What? That's impossible, Claire. You had a dream, and you probably imagined it was me," he said as he walked over and wrapped his arms around me.

"No, it was you, Sam, and she got real nervous and took the phone from me."

"Babe, we just made love. Your emotions are all fired up. It would make sense that your mind, your subconscious, would project that person as me. Let's get back in bed. You have a big day with your MRI and we need some sleep."

We climbed into bed and he wrapped his arms around me as I nestled my back into him. I didn't sleep at all, because I knew I was right. My mind was running a mile a minute, trying to put the pieces together. His accident was three years ago. My accident was three years ago. Both of us losing our memories. This wasn't a coincidence.

\*\*\*\*

I hated MRIs. The confinement, not being able to move, the clanking noise of the machine. It bothered me, but I'd had so many of them since the accident, I knew what to expect. Sam waited for me with Dr. Benjamin on the other side of the glass. When I was finished, I got dressed and waited in the waiting room with Sam for Dr. Benjamin. I kept looking at my phone, hoping Rachel would call, but she didn't and every time I tried to call her, it went to voicemail. Dr. Benjamin called us into his office and motioned for us to have a seat.

"I've looked over your MRI, Claire, and you have a lot of scar tissue, which I believe is causing your headaches. Frankly, I'm surprised you haven't had any seizures."

"What can you do for her, doctor?" Sam asked.

"I can go in and remove the scar tissue and hope for the best. But, I'm going to be honest, Claire, from the reports I saw from your accident, and the trauma you suffered, it's a miracle you're here."

"I was sent back. The woman said it wasn't my time," I spoke as I looked down.

Sam's eyes widened and Dr. Benjamin continued to look at me. "Let's schedule the surgery when you get back from your trip," he said as he closed his folder and walked out of the office.

"What do you mean you were 'sent back'?" Sam asked as he grabbed my hand.

I looked at him. "Not here. Let's go somewhere else."

I got up, walked out of the office, and out of the hospital. I climbed into Sam's car as he asked where I wanted to go. It had started raining again, typical Seattle weather, but I didn't care.

"I want to go to the beach."

Sam looked at me like I was crazy. "Claire, it's raining."

"I know, but that's where I want to go."

He let out a big sigh. "Okay, to the beach it is, in the pouring down rain."

As soon as he parked the car, I got out and ran toward the water. Sam followed behind me. I turned and looked at him as the rain fell down on us, drenching our skin and clothes.

"You wanted to know what I meant back at the hospital. Well, here it is. I saw my body lying in the hospital bed, and then I was in a garden filled with flowers. A woman stood before me in a long, white gown and told me it wasn't my time and that the road to recovery was going to be long and painful. Then she said if your love was really true, you would find each other again."

Sam just stood there, staring at me.

"I've never told anyone that."

"You said you didn't have a boyfriend."

"I didn't, or at least that's what everyone told me. Sam, don't you get it? I think it was you. Your car accident, my car accident, both of us losing our memories. We lived twenty minutes away from each other. Put it together, Sam."

He stood there in the rain with his hands on his hips, looking away from me. "It's a coincidence, Claire, that me and you were both in a car accident. I would have remembered you, for fuck's sake."

"You said you didn't remember a year of your life prior to the accident. What if we dated that year and you don't remember?"

I couldn't tell if the water on Sam's face was from the rain or tears. "NO! My mom said I wasn't dating anyone prior to the accident and my mom has never lied to me," he yelled. "I'm done with this, Claire. I think you're trying to make yourself believe things that aren't real or never happened so you can feel better about yourself."

My heart sank and I felt weak. His words stung me like a bee sting. I looked at him, shook my head, and then started running. The tears that filled my eyes mixed with the rain falling down my face. I couldn't breathe; it was too much. I felt like my world was closing in on me. The one person I trusted with my life and he couldn't find it in his heart to believe me.

"Claire, get back here. Where are you going?" He started to chase after me and, being more fit than I, he tackled me to the ground and we both fell onto the wet sand.

"Let go of me!" I screamed and struggled to loosen his grip on me.

"No, you're not running from me. I love you, Claire Montgomery. I love you so much it hurts."

I stopped struggling when I heard his words. He loosened his grip on me and I turned to face him, grabbing his face and kissing him fiercely. "I love you too, Sam Snow." And there it was, those three words that made him mine. Sam smiled as he hovered over me.

"Are you sure, Claire?"

"I've never been so sure of anything in my life." I smiled.

"Then we need to figure this out but you can't keep thinking that I was the one with you three years ago. It's just not possible."

I could sense the pain in his voice. Sam was scared to death that I was right and now I knew I'd have to find out the truth on my own. I didn't want to cause him anymore pain. He gave me one last kiss and then helped me up from the sand. We walked hand in hand back to the car.

"Good thing you have leather seats," I laughed.

"No shit. Let's go home and take a hot shower."

I leaned over to him and kissed his cheek. "I'm sorry, Sam." He pulled my head closer and stroked my wet hair.

"We'll figure this out together. I promise," he said as he kissed the top of my head.

# *Chapter 15*

We packed up the car for our road trip back to California. Ida looked out her window, smiling at us and waving goodbye. I gave her a wave, got into the car, and fastened my seat belt. I looked over at Sam, who was wearing light-colored jeans with a slight hole in the knee and a black, tight-fitted t-shirt. His light brown hair was tousled perfectly and he had on his black Ray Bans. He looked over at me as I stared at him.

"Why are you staring at me?" He smiled.

"Because I'm so in love with you."

He reached over and stroked my cheek with his hand. "I'm so in love with you too, baby."

I popped in a Joshua Radin CD and we sang duets together. It was only us and the open road. I sat and looked out the window, giving thought to everything that was going on. As soon as I reached Newport Beach, I was going to find out the truth of my life before the accident, and I was going to start with Rachel and Ally.

"Are you hungry, babe?" Sam asked as he patted my thigh.

"Yeah, I am. Is there anywhere close to stop?"

There was a sign up ahead with a list of restaurants. My phone chimed with a text from Ally.

*"Hi, Claire. I'm super excited you're coming home for the shower. I can't wait to see you."*

I smiled as I typed my reply.

*"I can't wait to see you either."*

Little did she know it was going to be on my terms, and my terms only. Nobody knew I was driving back with Sam. As far as everyone was concerned, I was flying. Harry offered to pick me up from the airport, but I told him Ally and Rachel were picking me up so we could have some girl time.

Sam pulled into McDonalds. "Is this okay, babe? I'm really craving a Big Mac."

I laughed. "It's fine. I like McDonalds."

I didn't care where we ate; I just needed to get out of the car and stretch my legs. We sat in a booth, ate our burgers, and headed back on the road. I fell asleep for a while and woke suddenly to the bright flashing lights going off in my head. I grabbed my head.

"Sam!" I screamed.

He immediately pulled over to the side of the road as I rocked back and forth and tears fell from my eyes. He got out of the car and opened the passenger door. He grabbed me and held me tight.

"Breathe through it, Claire. It will be over with soon."

The lights stopped flashing and my mind turned black. As I loosed the grip on my head, I took in a deep breath.

"Is it over, babe?"

I nodded my head and he let go of me and kissed my lips. He reached into my purse and got out my pills.

"Here, take this," he said as he handed me the pill and his pop.

I could tell Sam was tired. We left a day early so we could stop overnight.

"You look tired, honey. Let's find a hotel and get some rest."

"I think I saw a sign that there's a hotel in a couple of miles. We'll stay there," he said.

"Just make sure it's a nice hotel first. I don't want to stay in some motel out of a horror flick."

He threw back his head and laughed. "I'll see what I can do, babe."

I loved when he called me babe and baby. It felt so right and gave me tingles every time he said it. We found a hotel that met my needs. It was the third hotel we drove to. Sam inserted the key card and opened the door. I walked in and set my bag down. I turned to Sam, lifted his shirt off, and started to unbutton his jeans.

"What are you doing, Miss Montgomery?" He smiled.

I softly pressed my lips to his neck and nibbled on his ear.

"I know you're tired, so let me do the work."

I worked off his jeans and then his black boxers. I wrapped my hand around his erection, softly stroking it up and down while I guided him to the bed. Soft groans escaped his throat as I pushed him down and stripped for him. He pushed himself up to the pillows as I climbed on top of him, kissing his lips. As I hovered over him, he fondled my breasts and pulled at my erect nipples. He took each breast in his mouth and sucked with passion.

"Come up here and let me get you wet," he whispered.

I scooted up to him as he licked my aching spot and sucked me lightly, making sure I was ready for him. I could feel myself swell, so I moved down and softly grabbed his cock and guided him into me. He moaned and moved his hips up to reach deep inside me. I sat up and rode him up and down, clasping his chest with my hands. He kept his hands on my hips pushing, me down as I went around in circles. We both were ready to come as we both moaned and I gushed all over him, causing him to explode inside me. I collapsed onto him and buried my face into his neck. As my breathing began to slow down, the pain in my head emerged and bolts of bright lights filled my mind.

"Ah!" I yelled as I rolled off of him and grabbed my head. "Fuck!"

Sam immediately sat up and grabbed a hold of my arms. He knew to let me just ride it out because there was nothing he could do. Flashes of a bed and me lying in someone's arms flipped through my mind. We were both naked. I closed my eyes tighter, trying to focus on the man next to me, but I couldn't see his face. Suddenly, the pain was gone, the lights were gone, and so was the image. I let go of my head and fell into Sam's arms.

"I wasn't a virgin," I said.

"What?"

I looked up at Sam's face. "I wasn't a virgin. The flashes I just had were of me and someone lying in a bed."

He pulled me into him and sighed. "It doesn't matter to me whether or not you were a virgin. What matters is that we're together and we're going to get through this."

I knew deep down in my heart that he was one with me before the accident. I could feel it every time he touched me.

****

The next morning, we hopped back on the I-5 S and headed out of Oregon. It wouldn't be too much longer before we arrived in California. I put up my feet on the dash as we listened and sang along to Queen. Sam was looking extra sexy because he hadn't shaved in a couple of days and he had that sexy man scruff going on. I took my hand and rubbed it. I was finding it very difficult to keep my hands off him. He turned his head and looked at me with a wide grin.

"You like that?"

"I love it." I smiled.

All of a sudden, something hit me. "Oh shit, I never got Zoey a baby gift."

"How did you forget that?"

"Gee, I wonder, Sam. You've been a huge distraction."

He laughed. "Oh, so it's my fault you didn't get your sister a baby gift?"

"Yeah, maybe if you weren't so damn sexy and so loveable, I would be able to think about other things."

He reached over and grabbed my hand. "I know the feeling, babe. Don't worry. As soon as we get into California, we'll stop and buy something."

I stared out the window, in deep thought, while biting down on my bottom lip.

"You okay, Claire?"

"I'm just a little nervous about seeing my family, that's all."

Sam put his hand on my thigh. "I know, but if you want, I'll come with you."

"You know how much I love you, right?" I asked.

"Yeah, of course."

"I don't know if I'm ready for you to meet the Montgomery family. I still have questions left unanswered and it could get ugly."

"It's okay. I understand, but I do want you to meet my mom."

I looked at him and smiled while taking hold of his hand. "I can't wait to meet her."

We were just a short drive to Newport Beach. "My iPhone says the nearest Babies R Us is in five miles."

"I know. Remember, I lived here too." He smiled.

*Just another coincidence, right?*

We pulled into the parking lot and walked hand in hand into the store. I pulled Zoey's registry up from the computer and glanced at it.

"Oh my God. All that for one baby?" Sam exclaimed as he looked at it with me.

"I guess so. Good thing she lives in a big house."

"I think you might have waited too long, Claire. It looks like everything's been bought."

I shrugged my shoulders. "That's okay. I'll get her some baby clothes."

We walked over to the clothes section and to the boys' area. Zoey was having a boy and I could tell she was secretly disappointed. I was at one rack and Sam was at another. He was so cute, looking through the sleepers and holding them up for my opinion. It made me think that maybe one day we'd be doing this for our baby. Okay, I was getting ahead of myself, but the thought did pop into my mind.

"Claire, is that you?" I heard someone familiar.

I turned around, and across the aisle were Rachel and Ally.

"Eek, it is you," Ally squeaked as she ran over and almost knocked me down.

Rachel followed and the three of us shared a big girlfriend hug.

"What are you guys doing here?" I asked.

"Last minute shopping for your sister's shower," Rachel answered.

Sam strolled over and put his hand on the small of my back. Ally and Rachel gasped and Ally covered her mouth with her hand.

"Rachel, Ally, this is Sam Snow, my boyfriend."

I noticed the strange reaction and the looks on Ally's and Rachel's faces, and then I got a sick feeling in my stomach.

"Hi, nice to meet you both." Sam smiled as he extended his hand.

Both girls stuttered and acted nervous.

"What's going on with you two?" I asked.

"Nothing, Claire. It's just that your boyfriend is incredibly sexy and we're so happy to see you with someone," Ally said.

Sam blushed and looked down.

Rachel looked at her phone. "Shit, look what time it is. Ally we're late for that thing. We have to go."

"Okay, well, I will see you guys tomorrow at the shower. Please do me a favor and don't tell my parents or Zoey about Sam. I want it to be a surprise."

"No worries, Claire. Our lips are sealed," Ally said.

As they walked away, I could see something in their faces as they whispered to each other.

"That was a little uncomfortable," Sam said.

"Yeah, no kidding. Something is going on with them. They know something."

I paid for the baby items and we walked back to the car. Sam looked over at me as he fastened his seat belt. "I'll drop you off at home and then go to my mom's house."

My face turned sad. "I can't bear to be without you tonight."

Sam ran his finger down my jawline, "I know, babe. I can't either."

"I want to meet your mom now. I don't want to go home first. In fact, can we get a hotel for the night and I'll go home tomorrow to attend the shower?"

Sam's face looked surprised. "Sure, I'll take you home with me now, but you better tell your mom you aren't coming today."

I pulled my phone out of my purse and dialed Corinne.

"Hi, Claire." She sounded stressed.

"Hi, Mom. I wanted to let you know that my flight was delayed, and I won't be in until tomorrow."

"What? Claire Rose Montgomery, you better not be late for your sister's shower."

Sam's eyes widened because I had her on speakerphone and she was yelling.

"Calm down, Mom. I'll be home in plenty of time before the shower, I promise."

"You better be, Claire; this is very important to your sister and Dylan."

"Bye, Mom." I rolled my eyes as I hit the end button.

"Wow, you would think the world revolves around Zoey," Sam said.

"Yeah, it pretty much does," I said seriously.

# Chapter 16

My stomach tied itself in knots as Sam pulled into the driveway of his mother's house. I took in a deep breath and got out of the car. Sam held my hand as we walked through the door.

"There's my boy," his mother said as she turned around and gasped.

Suddenly, she looked as white as a ghost. "Mom, are you okay?"

She stood there staring at me, frozen, like she'd seen a ghost.

"I'm fine, Sam. It's just I'm so happy you're here," she stuttered.

He walked over and hugged her. "Mom, this is Claire, the girl I told you about over the phone."

Tears started to fill her eyes as she put her hand over her mouth, unable to control the sobs that followed.

"Mom, what is it? What's wrong?" Sam took her hand and led her to the table so she could sit down.

I looked at them, horrified. "Sam, I think it's me."

"Don't be ridiculous, Claire."

I walked over to his mom and took her hand. "You know me, don't you?"

"Claire, that's enough!" Sam snapped as he walked over to the sink to get a glass of water.

"Mrs. Snow, please. I'm begging you."

Sam walked over to me. "Claire, I said enough!"

Just as he turned his back, his mother spoke. "She's right, Sam."

My jaw dropped and I instantly felt sick to my stomach. Sam turned around, tightened his jaw, and looked in his mother's direction. "What do you mean 'she's right'?"

She took in a sharp breath before she began to explain. "You and Claire knew each other before the accident, and it's by the grace of God that you found each other again."

I knew it. I was right. It was Sam all along. The other person in my visions, the man in the picture Rachel had; it was Sam every time. He walked over and sat down next to her, tears filling his eyes.

"What are you talking about, Mom? You told me I wasn't seeing anyone before the accident."

My heart started to ache and a dark sadness came over me.

"I'm so ashamed, Sam, and I beg you to forgive me," she pleaded.

I could see Sam getting more upset by the second. I put my hand on his arm.

"Sam, please let her explain."

"You're lucky she's here, Mom, or I would have left already and you would never see me again."

"The night of the accident, you went to pick up Claire because she got in a fight with her parents and she left home. You were bringing her back here to stay with us. You were stopped at a traffic light and, when the light turned green, you went, but two cars that were racing one another ran the light and smashed into you, causing you to spin and crash into another car. When Claire's parents found out she didn't remember anything about her life, they came to me and asked how you were. When I told them you had woken up and couldn't remember the year prior to the accident, they offered me money never to mention Claire to you."

I gasped and felt like I was about to pass out.

"I took the money for you, son; for your medical bills and for your future."

Sam ran his hands through his hair and got up from his seat.

"Do you have any idea the hell I've lived?" he screamed.

I took in a deep breath as he turned and looked at me. "Baby, I'm so sorry. Please forgive me," he cried as he wrapped his arms around me.

His mother got up and went to her room. A few moments later, she came back and set an envelope on the table.

"I took these from your phone and had them developed after the accident. I don't know why I did, but I did, and now I'm giving them to you. All I can ask is for both of you to forgive me."

Sam grabbed the envelope from the table. "Claire, let's go."

"Sam, I think—"

"Now, Claire!" His voice was angry. This was a side of him I had never seen before. "Mom, I just need some time."

He stormed out the door and I ran after him. We drove in silence until we found a hotel. We got out of the car and Sam checked us in. He still wouldn't look at me. I wanted so badly to throw my arms around him and hold him tight. He opened the door, threw down our bags, and grabbed me, pushing me up against the wall. He grabbed my wrists and pinned them above my head.

"Sam, don't," I whispered.

He stopped and looked at me with cold, sad eyes. "I need to fuck you, Claire." His pained eyes pleaded. I brought my hand to his face and nodded. He lifted my shirt over my head and tore the button off my jeans; he took down the straps of my bra, exposing my breasts, and he quickly took down my underwear. I unbuttoned his jeans as he helped me take them off. He grabbed my leg and put it around his waist as he thrust inside me, slamming me up against the wall with each thrust. Soft groans rumbled in the back of his throat as he buried his face into my neck and released himself inside me. Sam lifted his head and look at me as tears started to fall from his eyes. I grabbed his head and pulled it into my chest. I felt his shoulders move up and down as he cried into me, letting go all his emotion. I felt his pain, but I had cried so much, there wasn't anything left, and now I needed to be strong for him. I lifted his head and softly kissed his lips. I led him to the bed, where we both lay down and held each other.

"I'm sorry, Claire."

"Sorry for what, Sam?" This beautiful, caring man had nothing to be sorry for and it broke my heart that he was apologizing to me.

"I'm sorry for not believing you."

I gently stroked his face. "You have nothing to be sorry for. You have been here for me and loved me, even when you thought I was crazy."

Sam let out a light laugh. I crinkled my nose at him and kissed his lips. "The only thing that matters is we found each other again. How many people can say that?"

Sam interlaced our fingers. "I lost three years with you, and believe me, I will spend the rest of my life making it up to you."

He pulled me into him and held my head against his chest. "I just can't believe this, Claire. I'm still trying to wrap my head around the whole thing. How could our parents do that?"

"Correction. You mean, how could *my* parents do that? I will never forgive them for this. What they did is unforgivable and I always knew something wasn't right."

**\*\*\*\***

The next morning, we got up, took a shower, and got dressed. Sam walked over to me as I was putting the final touches on my makeup.

"I didn't hurt you last night, did I?" he asked with great concern.

I turned and looked at him. "No, baby, you didn't hurt me at all. In fact, it was really hot."

He gave me that heart-melting smile and laughed. "Okay, then we'll have to try it more often."

"You better, Mr. Snow," I said as I tapped his nose with my blush brush.

He kissed my cheek and pulled out the envelope his mother gave him from his back pocket. He slowly opened it and removed several photos. He sat down on the edge of the bed and looked at them, one by one. As he looked up at me, he smiled and held up a picture of us kissing. I walked over and sat down next to him. I laid my head on his shoulder as he showed me each picture of us. We looked so happy and so in love, just like we were now.

"My parents kept us apart, Sam."

"It doesn't matter anymore, babe. Look, we found each other again, and this time, nothing and no one will ever tear us apart," he said as he kissed my head.

"You're right, but my parents will pay for what they did to us."

"We need to get going, Claire," he said as he handed me the pictures.

Sam gathered his wallet and keys. We left the hotel and he drove me to the house. I twisted my hands the whole way, knowing I had to put on an act until the shower was over. Sam reached over and stroked my hair.

"Stay strong, baby."

I took his hand and kissed his palm. "Don't worry; strong is all I am now."

I walked through the front doors of the Montgomery house and was greeted by a server with a tray of mimosas. I took a glass and downed it as fast as I could. The foyer was decorated with arrangements of fresh flowers. I walked to the kitchen, where a chef and his team were preparing the food. Waiters and waitresses graced the backyard, making sure the guests were taken care of. I walked out the patio door.

"Claire, darling," Corinne spoke as she hugged me. "Welcome home, darling."

"Hi, Mom." I kissed her on the cheek.

"Claire, you look fabulous," Zoey said as she hugged me and then whispered, "You have some explaining to do."

I rolled my eyes and whispered back, "You have no idea."

In the middle of the backyard, there was a large white tent decorated with white lights. Inside the tent sat round tables with white and light blue linens. Fresh flower arrangements of blue carnations and white roses decorated the tables with fine white china that was perfectly placed. One side of the tent was lined with tables made for gifts as the other housed a cake table and multiple cupcake towers.

"Claire, honey." Harry walked up to me with open arms.

"Hi, Dad. How are you?"

"I'm good, sweetheart. How are you? You look amazing."

I gently smiled when I heard Rachel and Ally calling my name. I turned and looked at them.

"Go talk to your friends. I'm sure you have a lot of catching up to do," Harry said as he kissed my cheek and walked away.

I stood there and waited for them to approach me. Ally came running to me with her arms open as Rachel slowed behind her. We hugged and pretended nothing had happened yesterday at the store. The shower was about to start when Corinne got up and made a speech.

****

After four hours and about a few hundred gifts later, the guests started to rise from their seats and leave. Zoey and Dylan were beaming from ear to ear as they looked over the generous presents people gave them. I sent a text message to Sam.

*"The shower is ending. It's time for you to come over and meet my parents again."*

*"I'll be there soon. Are you okay?"*

*"I've never been better. Just hurry. I'll wait for you out front."*

*"On my way, babe."*

Sam pulled up and got out of the car. I walked over to him, grabbed his hand, and led him through the backyard to the tent. My family and friends were in there, cooing over the baby clothes. "Mom, Dad, I want you to meet the love of my life." They turned around and their faces dropped as they looked at Sam.

"This is Sam, Sam Snow." Rachel grabbed a hold of Ally's arm as both girls stood frozen in time, waiting for the show to begin. Sam extended his hand to my parents.

"Hi, Mr. and Mrs. Montgomery. It's nice to finally meet you."

Harry smiled and, for the first time, Corinne was speechless. Her lips parted. "How did you two meet?" she stuttered.

I grabbed Sam's arm and leaned into him. "He lives in the apartment across the hall from me."

Corinne grabbed Harry's arm and held on for dear life. Zoey stood there, hanging onto Dylan. She looked like she was about to go into labor. Silence filled the tent, which alerted me that I had everyone's attention.

Corinne shifted uncomfortably in her position as Harry looked away. I looked around the tent. "Is there something anyone has to tell me?"

Sam looked at me and leaned closer; he knew what was about to happen. "How about you, Mother, Father, Zoey?" I glared at them.

I let go of Sam and walked closer to my parents, circling them as I spoke. "What was I doing before the accident? Who was I with? Can anyone tell me?"

Corinne looked at me with a stern look. "Claire, we've been over this a thousand times."

"You're right, Corinne." Her eyes widened. "We have been over this a thousand times and it's been nothing but a thousand lies," I shouted in her face. "It seems to me that Sam and I didn't just meet in Seattle. We were dating before the accident and you forbade me to see him anymore, so I packed up and left home, except I didn't get very far, now, did I, Mother?"

Tears swelled in her eyes. "Claire, that's enough," Harry snapped.

I looked away from Corinne and into my father's eyes. "I'm not even close to being done, Dad, and of all people, I thought I could trust you." His face took on pain and his eyes slowly closed.

"How could you do this to me? I'm your daughter, your flesh and blood, and you destroyed my life."

Corinne looked at me and clenched her jaw. "No, he destroyed your life," she said as she pointed to Sam.

I gasped. "It was an accident and it could have happened to anybody. You destroyed my life the minute you forbade me to see him. If you had only accepted me and him, the accident wouldn't have happened, so you have no one to blame but yourself, you bitch," I screamed in her face.

Corinne raised her hand and slapped me across the face. Sam gasped and lunged toward me. I threw my arm back to block him as Harry grabbed Corinne and held her. Zoey took a few steps forward, but Dylan held her back. I held the side of my face, which stung from her hand.

"Feel better now, Corinne? Silly woman, you thought because you have money and influence that you could keep Sam and me apart? But guess what, Corinne, the universe had other plans for us and we were meant to find one another again."

Zoey spoke up. "She's right, Mom."

I looked at her in anger and pointed my finger. "You are supposed to be my sister. How could you lie to me like that?" The bright lights started to flash in my mind, like someone was taking pictures with the flash on. I grabbed my head and knelt to the ground as tears fell down my face. Sam wrapped his arms around me from behind and sat on the floor with me.

"Breathe, baby, don't fight it," he whispered as he kissed my head. Corinne and Harry ran over to me. "Stay away from her," Sam yelled as he looked up at them.

"How dare you? That's my daughter," Corinne snapped in anger.

"You don't have a clue about your daughter and what she goes through. You're not there, helping her through these excruciating headaches."

Harry knelt down in front of me. "Claire, sweetheart, let us help you."

I smiled as the images stopped and the lights dissipated. Sam loosened his grip and helped me up. I turned around to face him with the smile that never left my mouth.

"I saw you, us, on the beach. We were watching the sunset and sitting on a blanket. You packed us subs; in fact, you brought a bunch of them because you didn't know what I liked. I remembered that moment, Sam," I cried as he hugged me and kissed me softly on the top of my head.

"You're going to remember a lot more," he whispered.

I turned back around to face my family and friends. It was time to say goodbye. Everyone was crying. "What each one of you in this room has done to me and Sam is unforgivable. You each had a part in making the last three years of my life a living hell." I pointed my finger to each person in the tent. "You could have told me about Sam and we could have tried to reconnect, but you didn't; you hid it like some dirty little secret and, for that, I will never forgive you. Consider me dead to all of you because that's what you all are to me. Now, if you'll excuse me, I have a life to go live." I took Sam's hand and walked towards the entrance of the tent.

Corinne screamed, "Claire, no, please don't do this! We love you."

Ally and Rachel ran out into the yard after us. "Please, Claire, Sam, please, we're sorry."

I stopped dead in my tracks and whipped my body around to face them. "You call yourselves my best friends? I forgot you once and I can easily do it again. You chose Corinne's side after the accident instead of mine. Even when I called you and begged you to tell me the truth, you still wouldn't. You're no friends. You're spineless little bitches, and I never want to see either of you again."

Ally and Rachel both started crying. Harry walked over to me and pleaded with me not to leave.

"I'm sorry, Dad, but you and the rest of this family have nobody to blame but yourselves. What you did by keeping secrets and telling me lies about my past is unforgiveable. You and mom let me think that I was driving and that someone died in my car. You think your money and your influence can control people. Well, you know what, Harry? You failed. You may be able to buy off people and keep them silent, but you can't control fate and the universe. All of you need to take a good look at yourselves in the mirror and ask God for forgiveness. When I died in that hospital bed, a woman came to me in a garden and told me that if our love was true, we'd find our way back to each other. That's something you can't ever silence. You're all pathetic."

I shook my head and Sam put his arm around me. There were no more tears that could fall from my eyes. As I turned around and started to walk away, I could hear Corinne sobbing. Zoey grabbed my arm and spun me around.

"Don't do this, little sister. I know we've had our differences in the past, but we can be different now. My baby is going to need you in his life. Please don't walk away from us."

I looked at her and gently placed my hand on her cheek. "Even though I can't remember what our relationship used to be before the accident, I get the feeling you hated me. To be honest with you, Zoey, I don't want to be around and watch a selfish bitch like you ruin your son's life. Enjoy being a mom and a senator's wife. You learned from the best and you deserve everything that will come your way," I said as I looked at Corinne.

Sam kissed my head and pulled me into him. I turned my back to them and, as I was walking away, I stuck my hand up and waved.

"Goodbye, Montgomery family."

# *Chapter 17*

Sam and I climbed in his car and he drove around the corner and threw the car in park. He turned his body so he was facing me and grabbed my hand.

"You are an amazing woman. What you did back there took a lot of strength and courage. I love you so much, Claire Montgomery." He smiled.

I took in a deep breath before I leaned over and softly kissed his lips. "You're the one who gives me strength, Sam. Being with you is the best thing that ever happened to me, again." I smiled. "I want to and need to remember our time together before the accident and the only person who can help with that is your mom."

"Claire, I'm not ready to—"

"Shh…" I said as I put my finger over his lips. "Your mom was worried about your medical bills and your future. She did what she had to in order to help you. Corinne and Harry are very convincing people. Why do you think she kept an envelope with our pictures in it? Because she knew that someday, we'd find each other again. You need to go and make things right with her. Tell her you forgive her and tell her how much you love her. You're all she has, Sam."

He looked down as a tear fell from his eye. "You're right. Will you come with me?" he asked.

"I wouldn't have it any other way." I smiled before kissing him again.

Sam took in a deep breath, put the car in drive, and drove to his mom's house. As we pulled up in the driveway, she was in the front, planting some flowers. She turned around and smiled when she saw us. We got out of the car as she took off her gardening gloves. Sam walked to her and wrapped his arms around her, hugging her tightly. Tears started to roll down her face as she kept apologizing over and over again.

"It's okay, Mom," Sam said.

"No, Sam, it's not okay. What I did was wrong and I'm so ashamed."

My phone kept ringing and ringing. I pulled it out of my purse and saw that I had missed calls from Harry, Zoey, Ally, and Rachel. I turned off my phone. The first thing I was going to do when I got back to Seattle was buy a new phone with a new number.

"Everything okay?" Sam asked me.

"Everything's good." I smiled.

Sam walked his mom into the house and I followed behind. She had just made some chocolate chip cookies and fresh lemonade. She asked Sam to put the plate of cookies on the table while she went and got something. A few moments later, she walked out with a phone and handed it to Sam.

"This is the phone you had before the accident. It has some pictures on it, but I want you to see all the text messages you sent back and forth to each other. I'm going to go back outside and finish planting those flowers while you two look through them and see what your life was like before the accident."

"Why did you save this stuff, Mom?"

She placed her hand on his cheek and smiled. "Because I had hoped that someday you'd find each other again and you'd want to know."

"I love you, Mom."

"I love you too, Sam. If you need me, I'll be outside."

Sam and I sat down on the couch and started looking through his phone. We started with the pictures. Even though the screen had a crack in it, we could see the pictures clearly. There were only a few pictures of us that his mom didn't get developed. There were a lot of pictures at the beach, my graduation, and at a park with Ally and Rachel. I put my head on Sam's shoulder as he pointed to our silly faces and we laughed. He began scrolling through the text messages. As we read them, tears started to fall down my face. Just to read his words and my words back was enough to show how much we cared and loved each other.

*"I'm going to marry you one day, Claire, and we'll have our own snow babies."*

*"You better, Sam Snow, and I'm holding you to that, forever!"*

*"I promise you a perfect forever, babe."*

*"And I promise you a perfect forever, my love."*

I lifted my head as Sam wiped the tears from my eyes. "These messages still hold true. They are our past, present, and future, Claire," he said as he kissed my lips.

I wrapped my arms around him and buried my face into his neck. "We're right where we're supposed to be."

We got up from the couch and walked outside. Sam and I knelt down next to his mom and helped her plant the rest of the flowers. She looked at us with a smile and nodded her head.

This life. The life I was supposed to have all along was finally mine. I wasn't part of a person anymore. Now, I was whole. My heart and soul had been filled. Filled with love and kindness by a man who was meant to be mine since the day we both were born. No accident could stand in the way of us being together. God had a plan for the two of us and he made sure we found each other once again. This timeline of life we ride is unknown, and now I know that everything happens for a reason; Sam being my reason for my survival, and me being his reason for his.

Thank you for reading. I hope you enjoyed Sam & Claire's story.

## *About The Author*

Sandi Lynn is a New York Times, USA Today and Wall Street Journal bestselling author who spends all of her days writing. She published her first novel, Forever Black, in February 2013 and hasn't stopped writing since. Her addictions are shopping, romance novels, coffee, chocolate, margaritas, and giving readers an escape to another world.

Please come connect with her at:

www.facebook.com/Sandi.Lynn.Author

www.twitter.com/SandilynnWriter

www.authorsandilynn.com

www.pinterest.com/sandilynnWriter

www.instagram.com/sandilynnauthor

https://www.goodreads.com/author/show/6089757.Sandi_Lynn

38482619R00092

Made in the USA
San Bernardino, CA
06 September 2016